I0784716

HOOKING TINK

HOLLY ROBERDS

BOOKS BY HOLLY ROBERDS

To the readers missing a piece of themselves—whether it's a chunk of heart, hope, or a literal hand.

You don't need to be whole to find love.

CHAPTER 1

YO, HO, BLOW ME DICK OFF

HOOK

Walking into a tattoo parlor, one doesn't expect to find an eight-year-old girl getting inked.

Yet that's exactly what I see when I step into Inked by Tink, escaping the wicked storm that crashes down on the streets of Boston. One more second out there and it would've blown my dick off.

I don't fancy replacing that appendage with a hook like I've had to do with my hand.

In contrast to the neon sign outside, the inside is warmly lit by lamps a floral-loving grandmother would favor. An entire wall is lined with celebrity photos, framed awards, and articles featuring the shop. The checkered tile floor is slick with rain, and the place is filled with a strange mix of odors: ink, antiseptic, and lilacs.

The little girl's eyes are squeezed shut as the artist leans over her arm, wielding the tattoo gun. The woman standing nearby, presumably the girl's mom, looks up at my entrance. The mother's eyes widen and her arms fall from where they were wrapped around her torso.

That's right, lady. A bad man just entered the building, but you have nothing to fear. For now.

I attempt a grin to put her at ease, but it feels unnatural and forced. The woman recoils, a hand shooting out to shield the little girl from me.

My smile twists into a sneer, then fades.

"Take a seat. I'll be with you in a minute," comes the melodic, feminine voice of the tattoo artist, even as she continues to focus on the child's arm. "Just a little longer," she murmurs to the girl. "You're doing great, Libby."

The child nods, still refusing to open her clenched eyes. Libby's chest jerks with ragged, uneven breaths.

Anger coils in me like a serpent preparing to strike. Why are they putting this kid through such pain? Part of me wants to fly forward, rip the tattoo artist off the girl, and get her the fuck out of here, away from these sadists.

But I'm here for a bloody reason and I refuse to jeopardize that. I run my fingers along the cold steel of my hook to distract and keep myself from doing something rash that could ruin my chances. I've waited fifteen long years to get here.

The sharp edge digs into the pad of my finger until I break the skin. Instantly, a fraction of my tension is relieved. I pop the digit in my mouth and the copper taste of my blood slides on my tongue like a comforting old friend. Despite cleaning my hands recently, I taste the permanent salty brine of the ocean on my skin.

A massive waterfall of platinum waves spilling from the back of her ponytail is all I can see of the tattoo artist. There must be more hair than body to the petite woman.

Tinkerbell.

It has to be her.

Wings stretch behind her, intricate as latticework, each

translucent panel shimmering with iridescent greens and purples. The frame is composed of chitin, the same tough material found in the exoskeletons of insects, giving them a strength that belies their airy appearance. Each movement is a dance of light and shadow.

The fleeting thought of how much her wings would go for on the black market briefly crosses my mind.

Boston is primarily a human city, but the little sprite decided to open her shop smack dab in the middle.

It almost piques my interest, but Tink's background isn't relevant. I clench my jaw in frustration, knowing I have no choice but to rely on her.

Impatience keeps me from sitting on the plush rose-colored loveseat, not the fact I'm sopping wet. The cold bites its way to the marrow of my bones. At least in the tropics, the rain has the decency to be warm. Boston is colder than a witch's tit, and I resent it.

I lean against the wall and do the only thing I can. Wait.

The mother's attention has returned to the little girl, lightly touching the tiny arm that clutches a stuffed bunny. The kid is too skinny, too pale. There's a gray tint to her skin, and blue veins are visible under her nearly translucent skin. Her warm brown hair is wispy and thinning, patches of scalp peeking through.

My stomach sloshes like a ship tossed by merciless salty waves.

Libby is sick. I recognize the signs. The plastic hospital bracelet encircling her wrist means it's likely serious.

The air around Tink and Libby begins to shimmer with a faint, golden light. Shimmering motes of pixie dust flicker in the air like glitter. I'm tempted to step toward the warmth of the energy, but I stay rooted to the spot.

The child's pallor fades, replaced by a healthy flush. Her

breathing steadies, and the tension in her shoulders slowly but surely eases.

"There," Tink says, silencing the buzz of the tattoo gun. "All done."

Libby's eyes open, revealing big brown depths. Her lips part in awe as she looks down at her arm. "That wasn't so bad." Then she lifts her arm to observe the design closer. "It's beautiful. I feel...better."

Tink brushes a strand of errant hair behind an ear lined entirely in silver studs, dangling jewels, and sparkling hoops. "The magic knows what you need," she says modestly, though her wings flutter in what I imagine to be unrestrainable delight. "This will help you stay strong. All you need is faith, trust, and pixie dust." Tink shoots a wink as she says the last bit before cleaning and wrapping the fresh design.

That little chestnut is more worthless than a ship with a hole in its hull.

Faith.

Trust.

Bloody hell. What a croc. Both are useless and if the girl had an ounce of common sense, she'd stick her chubby middle finger up at the pint-sized adult.

Though I can't deny I'm here for the pixie dust. Faith and trust come and go with the amount of green that passes hands.

The child's mother, who has been watching anxiously, picks her kid up from the adult-sized chair, holding her. Tears stream down her face. "Thank you." Her voice is choked with emotion. "You've given us hope."

The mom goes to grab her purse while Tink wipes off her equipment. When the sprite turns and stands, I get my first look at the only creature in this world who can help me. It's like a hot poker has been rammed under my ribs. Like her wings, she is a contrast in strength and fragility I'm instantly captured by.

At full height, Tinkerbell is barely over five feet tall. Her bird-like limbs are all covered in intricate tattoos. Thick, black glasses frame bright emerald eyes with pupils ringed in aquamarine. Smoky eye makeup heightens the gradation of color to a damn near supernaturally luminous glow. A silver ball stud sits just above her lips, a piercing I find difficult to understand the placement of. With the polka-dotted handkerchief knotted around the top of her head, she looks like a vintage pin-up model crossed with a punk rock, goth girl. She pinches off her latex gloves and throws them in the trash without so much as a glance at me.

As Tink moves, her crop top shifts slightly, revealing a glint of metal. The jeweled belly button piercing catches the light and draws my eyes to the smooth expanse of her midriff.

My nether region stiffens with acute, unabashed interest.

The mother rifles in her bag while the girl continues to stare at her arm. It's a blooming oak tree with colorful curly limbs extending downward into thick, ornate roots. The tree of life.

"This is a little piece of my home, and now you'll carry magic around with you as you fight this bitch." Tink holds up her hand and receives a solid high-five from the little girl. The mother's face tenses, but she doesn't object to the cursing. "Remember, you're stronger than you think, and you hold more magic inside you than you even know."

The girl nods with the serious focus of someone being entrusted with the secrets of the universe.

When the mother opens her wallet, Tink waves her off. "No charge."

After her repeated offers to pay are rejected, the woman and her child pass by me to the door. Libby waves at me from over her mother's shoulder. I wave back with my hook. The little girl's mouth drops open in surprise. I can't tell if it's a fearful reaction before the door closes behind them and they disappear into the stormy night.

Anticipation sizzles its way through me as my heart takes off at a sprint. The time to break through my invisible shackles has finally come. The weight of these curses bears down on me more with each passing day, and only this little pixie can set me free.

"What do you want?" Tinkerbell asks before I can speak, her words as strained as a taut rubber band.

My shoulders roll back as I prepare for the fight of my life. And this time, I can't use my sword or hook. I'll have to rely on my...charm.

Poseidon, help me.

CHAPTER 2

HOW TO NOT STAB SOMEONE FOR WHAT YOU WANT

HOOK

"What do you want?" Tink asks again.

"I'm—"

"I know who you are." The petite fairy crosses her arms, and I swear I almost see lightning crackling in her luminous green eyes. "James T. Hook." She spits my name out like it's a curse.

Half my mouth curls up. "I was *going* to say I'm impressed." I gesture to where she worked her magic on the kid. "And that would be *Captain* James T. Hook."

Tink rolls her eyes and cocks a hip like a gun.

The way she dismisses me, like I'm beneath her, grates on my nerves. She possesses the righteousness of the young and fearless who don't know to tread lightly around dangerous men.

And yet, blood rushes south with tingles of desire. Her impetuous attitude is getting me hard. Or maybe it's that pouty pink mouth or the electricity in her eyes. She's a live wire, and I'm tempted to grab hold of her and let her burn me.

Batten the hatches, Hook. That's not why you're here.

I adjust my stance in an attempt to ease the pressure building in my dick.

"I'm in need of your expertise." The words burn in my throat. For a moment, I almost made a plea for her help, but I know better than to appeal to a fae's compassion.

Tink's wings brush the air with a faint shimmer as she turns to tie off a trash bag as if to clean up for the night. "Well, that's too bad because I'm closed. Especially to men who murder, steal, and terrorize fae creatures for their treasures."

She won't give me the time, so like the pirate I am, I'll have to take it. Just like I do with everything else.

"I am marked by mermaids." I take a step forward, closing some of the distance between us, the urgency of my words pushing me closer. "Cursed by three she-demons of the deep." And my life has been a living hell ever since.

Tink's eyes narrow and she steps back slightly, bumping into the counter. Her movements are quick, almost instinctive. She hasn't yet learned to hide her reactions.

"Aww, did the big, bad pirate get outsmarted by a few fish girls? How embarrassing for you." Tink's eyes narrow, a wicked smile playing at her lips.

Smart-mouthed little brat.

That perpetual smirk on her face—she's mocking me, taunting me.

If she were anyone else, her blood would be covering the floor. If I didn't need her skills so badly, I'd teach her that there are consequences for disrespecting a man like me.

I grip the edge of the counter, my knuckles white with restraint. "Fifteen years, pixie. Fifteen years I've been enduring a sailor's worst nightmare on the seas. You have no idea what it's like. Every voyage is like sailing along the edge of a knife. The weather, my crew, even the stars themselves—nothing can be trusted. And it's all because of these." I pop the few buttons keeping my shirt closed. My fingers brush against a cursed tattoo and I sweep a hand over the Three of Hearts tarot card emblazoned on my bare skin. The other two markings are out of sight but just as powerful and deadly.

Half-boxed in by me, Tink is at eye level with my exposed chest. She wets her bottom lip and the smell of lilacs intensifies. Then her gaze flies up to meet mine with heat and hate.

A bad man like me could bask in the warmth of her disdain for decades.

"Fifteen years of curses, huh?" She pauses, tapping her chin thoughtfully with a black glitter-painted nail, her eyes never leaving mine. "Sounds like karma finally caught up with you, Captain. Maybe you should've tried being less of an asshole."

My anger flares like gas striking a flame, and it takes all my power to stick to my appeal instead of teaching her a lesson about mouthing off.

Steady, old boy. She's not a conquest, even if she makes you feel like a younger man. Stick to the facts. Don't ravage that pouty little mouth until she submits.

"Only a skilled tattoo artist who can wield magic will be able to unlock the curses and free me. I need you to unlock one of the curses now, and then I'll return for the other two in time." The words force their way out through my gritted teeth, though I'm still thinking of throwing her on this counter and pulling her apart until she screams my name. Whether by violence or lust is the real question.

Tink's wings flutter with what could be irritation or mockery as she turns away from me. "Break your curses? Sorry, I'm all out of *fix entitled pirate's self-inflicted problems* ink today. Try again, never." She continues to clean up the shop. Tinkerbell has written me off, dismissing me with a flick of her wrist.

My hook twitches at my side. The urge to grab her, to force her compliance, is almost overwhelming. Brute force won't work here. I need her willing participation, and that realization almost burns worse than the curses themselves.

Taking a deep breath, I release my grip on the counter. "I can pay. Upfront."

Tink doesn't respond. She crosses over to a fringed lamp and clicks it off, plunging a corner of the shop into shadow.

"Giving away services like that can't help with your rent," I say, referring to the woman and child who just left. "I hear it's expensive around these parts."

"I'm not interested in selling myself to the devil, even if I did need the money," she says.

Thunder cracks then booms. The entire shop rattles and the remaining lights flicker.

"Not even for triple the price?" To prove my point, I reach into my jacket and pull out a thick wad of cash, slamming it on the checkout counter.

She barely glances at it.

Fae fucking witch titty buckets up an arsehole.

It's clear this chit won't be taken in by intimidation, but I'm beginning to suspect there might be another button I can press. I glance at the wall covered in accolades for her skill.

Grabbing the stack of bills, I shove them back in my pocket. "I suppose it's a blessing in disguise," I pretend to grumble. "I'll find someone better than you at another port."

I turn and walk toward the door, gambling everything on a bluff.

"Better than me?" comes her outraged squeak.

I stop, letting a dark grin curl my lips for a moment.

Gotcha, fairy.

Wiping away all expression, I turn to look at her with feigned indifference. "I mean, you didn't think you were the *only one* to corner the market on magic tattoos, did you, pixie?" My words drip with saccharine insult. The taunt pays off as her face turns red, a frown pulling at her pouty lips and eyes crackling with the promise of violence.

"I am the only game in *any* town, and I am the best," she announces with venom, closing the distance between us.

Lilacs assail me again, and I've never known flowers could make me so hard.

I scratch my jaw with my hook. "Did you really think you were the sole being with magical tattoo skills...in the world? There are others out there. More experienced. More talented." I'm lying, but I can't let her figure that out.

"You might be the best in this little town, but out there?" I shrug. "You're just a small fish in a big pond."

The way her lashes flutter with barely suppressed rage tells me I've punched her right in the pride yet again.

Tink closes the distance between us. Eyes blazing, cheeks flushed with anger, her delicate chin juts at an obstinate angle to meet my gaze. "I am the best," she snaps. Her wings twitch in agitation and her floral scent wafts over me in strong yet short spurts.

She seethes with a righteous fury that stokes the fire in my veins. We're toe to toe now, and all I can think about is how much I want to push her, break her defiance, and watch her crumble beneath me.

Fight her.

Fuck her.

Dominate her.

My primal desires claw at my chest, begging to be set loose. But I cling to self-control even as my muscles tense and my breaths come in short bursts. If she dares to deny me once more, I will have no choice but to unleash the beast within and take what I want by force.

And right now, there is nothing I need or want more than Tinkerbell.

"If you want to prove yourself, here's your chance. Break these curses, and you'll have bested the most powerful mermaids in the seven seas."

CHAPTER 3

THE APPEAL OF AN OLDER PIRATE

TINK

My pulse races with outrage at this pirate questioning my abilities.

I don't care if he is the scourge of the oceans, a name whispered in terror wherever ships sail. The tales of Captain Hook are well-known, his exploits legendary and soaked in blood. A pirate with a heart as cold as the steel of his hook, who has betrayed, manipulated, and destroyed countless fae creatures to line his pockets. He's the kind of man who would sell out a friend to save his own skin and think nothing of it. He's the type to charm his way through any blockade—or any bed—only to vanish by morning, leaving wreckage in his wake. Big scary pirate or not, he's crossed a line, and I plan to make him choke on his words.

I'll show him what I'm worth.

"Triple the price," I demand, trying to ignore how being this close to him feels like standing at the edge of a storm, waiting for lightning to strike.

I'm not in the habit of helping murderous pirates with reputations as black as the deepest ocean trenches.

Comparing him to a serial killer who pulls wings off pixies might be too kind.

So why am I agreeing to help him now?

It's a knee-jerk reaction, something that flares up whenever someone dares to doubt my skills. The very suggestion that he could find another artist better suited to this burns like acid in my brain, searing my thoughts and leaving a bitter taste in my mouth.

I've been dismissed countless times due to my size, gender, and my fae blood. Even now, at twenty-six, I have to fight to be taken seriously, especially by those who've seen more of the world. Like him.

Straight up, fuck all that.

My reputation is all I have and I'll be damned if I let anyone question it.

Hook's lips twitch as if he's suppressing a smile. With his stormy gaze and long, dark, curly hair dripping onto my nice tile floors, I'm almost certain he's the devil incarnate.

I should have known the devil would look like sin and temptation, with a voice that promises hell and hands that could pull me down willingly.

The idea of him leaving this shop, smug with the notion that I couldn't take on his curses, gnaws at me. I can hear him laughing with some other tattoo artist about that fairy in Boston who couldn't get the job done. It's not just about proving him wrong—it's about proving myself for the thousandth time.

When will it be enough? When will you *be enough?* The questions bounce around inside my head, as irritating as gnats.

I swallow hard knowing that day may never come. But I am more than capable of handling this 'scary' pirate and his petty curse problem.

"Before I agree to payment, I need to make sure you can do the job." Hook retrieves a ratty cloth from his coat pocket. Peeling back the layers of fabric, he reveals a crusty old skeleton key. "I'll need you to tattoo this likeness onto the curse itself."

I roll my eyes again, so hard they might fall out of my skull. "Oh yeah, this is a massive challenge." I reach to snatch the key out of his grasp, but he closes his fist and pulls it back protectively.

"You don't know what it took to get this." His voice is a low, raspy growl of pure menace as he leans in, eyes blazing with barely restrained violence.

A shiver races up my spine. My internal alarms are all going off with red blaring lights, announcing DANGER in all caps as he bears down on me.

I suddenly understand the appeal of the older man. He's not old enough to be my father, but certainly an uncle or second cousin, maybe? He has a dangerous allure, a seen-it-all kind of confidence. There is no doubt, no mystery as to what he wants or what he will do to get it.

Hook's dark, twisted expression is at odds with the seductive scent of the ocean mixed with a heady spice that screams male virility. It enfolds me, causing my center to melt like a piece of dark chocolate on a warmed skillet.

Girl, you are hard up if this is your reaction.

I've been so busy running the shop, I haven't had action in six months.

Well that, and the man-children around here don't want to grow up. They stay out partying all night only to do the bare minimum at their dead-end jobs so they can do it all over again.

I attract a very specific type. The type that thinks I have no ambition and want to stay young and free forever.

Fuck that. I'm out here hustling, living my purpose, running my own business. And never do I feel more alone than when attached to someone who says, *I don't believe in labels*, or *why can't we just keep having fun?*

No, thanks. I know what the fae fucks I want, and these noncommittal party boys are *not* it.

Still, the excuse of it being a while since I got laid doesn't explain how arresting I find the feral edges of Hook's sharp face. Piercing blue eyes set over a straight nose seem to slice through me as deeply as if he were using a cutlass.

It's not just his reputation; it's the way he carries himself, the way he looks at me like he's already imagining how to break me.

Realizing my breath is coming in a jerky rhythm and warmth is spreading too quickly through my body, I take a couple of steps back and move out of his gravitational pull.

"Go sit down in the back," I command, needing to regain control of the situation and my reaction to him. "I don't want anyone to know I'm taking such lowly clientele," I add, brushing by him to lock the front door.

The laugh that comes out of him is raspy and sardonic, and I don't care for how it hits me in the solar plexus like a literal blow before dribbling lower to my inexplicably melting parts.

I'm already regretting this deal.

STRIPPED of his long coat and shirt, Hook stands in my private back room. My mouth turns dry at the sight of his bare chest, and a tingling sensation burrows through me.

Captain James T. Hook, notorious pirate, plunderer, and

murderer is all lean, ropy muscle and deeply tanned skin. His posture screams arrogance, and it grates on me. Even half-naked, he's insufferable.

All men who have those deep cuts of muscles at their hips are insufferable.

I wipe the corner of my lips where moisture gathers. It's not drool. Definitely not.

I've tattooed all kinds of people on all different body parts. Hell, I've tatted a dude's nutsack before. This is no different than working with any other client.

The hot liquid sensation between my thighs suggests otherwise.

The faded ink of his many tattoos is decorated by the numerous chains and string necklaces that fall from his neck. There are strange gems, beads, and jagged teeth, likely harvested from lethal sea creatures.

Murderer, my common sense whispers.

It annoys me that he only looks more rugged with jewelry adorning him. Judging by the crow's feet framing his eyes and some strands of gray in his raven black hair, the man is maybe ten or twenty years older than me. Yet he is in far better shape than most of the men I go out with in Boston.

It doesn't matter, Tink. None of that matters. You need to focus on prepping the equipment.

"Sit," I direct, then attempt to slink around him to get to my cabinet drawers. Instead, he steps directly in front of me, forcing me to tilt my head back to meet his eyes.

"This won't be an ordinary tattoo." His voice is lower, softer, which only increases its rasp. His British accent strikes me in the lower belly, causing my inner muscles to clench.

My reaction only furthers my irritation. "Of course it won't be. Mine are always magic."

I try to get past him again but he grasps my wrist, keeping me in place. His calloused palm is surprisingly dry and warm. Arousal curls tighter in me immediately followed by a sick churning in my stomach.

I can't have this reaction. Not to Captain Hook. The pirate who slit a mermaid's throat so he could steal her most prized possession. The legend changes every time I hear it—how he killed her, how he lured or seduced her—but the basics remain the same.

He exploits and kills fae beings, which is sickening.

So why don't I feel sick?

All I can submit to him is that at least he has the decency to openly be the bad guy. The worst kind of villain is the one who pretends to be your friend, who lures you in before betraying you.

My acid-coated stomach clenches with the grief I've carried for so many years, it's become part of me.

"I need you to remember these aren't tattoos." He sweeps his hook over his torso, forcing my attention to them. "They are curses."

"I got it," I say, jerking out of his hold. My words came out a little less confident than I intended. His touch and the way his eyes pierce mine cause a riot of heat and desire in me, pushing aside the lingering pain of my past. "So where do we start, boss?" I ask sarcastically as I snap one of my gloves to alleviate some of my nervous energy.

Hook points to the tattoo covering the center of his chest.

Of course. I have to be right in his face. Couldn't start with one on his back.

Something light and hot races up my spine, so I glower at him harder.

"Lean back," I instruct. He may be older, scarier, and dangerous, but this is my house and that means I'm in charge.

Stepping on the pedals underneath, I adjust the seat, dropping him. I brush away his hair and his necklaces, causing his far too-inviting scent to wrap around me, making my insides turn to jelly. My lips tighten against the sensation.

One of his necklaces catches my eye. It's a curved turquoise likeness of a wave. Magic radiates from it with a barely audible thrum. As a fae, I've always been able to sense magic. But that's not my business, so I move the pendant aside.

Getting to the task at hand, I study the expanse of his chest. Covering it is the Three of Hearts.

"So this is a curse, huh?" Even I wouldn't have guessed. "Looks like a regular tattoo. Good work, nice artistry." I'm not sure if it's nerves or habit, but my mouth runs away with itself as I prep my tools. "I've tatted this one on people dozens of times. Three of Hearts from the tarot deck. It signifies grief, betrayal, and heartache. Some people want to keep their pain so close to them. I get it though. Hidden pains can rot. At least with them etched on skin they have a chance to be acknowledged or at the very least aired out."

To Hook's credit, he doesn't interrupt or snap at me for being chatty, which kind of surprises me. Instead, he watches me with intense scrutiny as if he's studying me.

My hand brushes along the lines of the marking. I may have underplayed the artistry of the ink. It's gorgeous. The jeweled hilts of the three swords are particularly ornate, the red of the anatomically correct heart and the blood on the sword points stabbing through it as bright as the day it was first tattooed on his skin.

For a moment, I swear I see a drop of blood fall from one of the blades before it reappears on its tip.

"Curses, not tattoos," Hook reminds me in a low, soft voice.

"Right." I swallow.

He lets out a low moan. Realizing my gloved fingers have been softly stroking and following the lines of the tattoo with my need to familiarize myself with it, I jerk back as if I've touched fire.

Keep it professional, Tink.

He's a bad, disgusting pirate. He tortures and steals from your kind and more.

I should be flaying him in the name of my kind, not helping him.

My palm opens. Hook hesitates a moment, but finally hands over the key.

"Where do you want it?" I ask.

His gaze digs into me, getting under my skin. I oddly fear I'll be branded by it long after he goes.

"I'm not sure." He licks his lips, and for some reason I find it devastatingly and unforgivably hot. "I was hoping you could use your fairy wiles to figure this out."

I tilt my head, trying to find gaps in the design.

If it's a key to unlock the curse, there must be some kind of hole or placement where it goes that would make sense.

Using the key itself, I lay it on his chest and twist it this way and that until a soft little click happens inside my body. It's not the magic of his curse—it's instinct.

Designs come to me, and when I find the thread of what it is supposed to be or where it is supposed to be located on my client's body, I intuit a click. Then I follow the cues like a ticking metronome until it's done, and I'm satisfied.

To Hook's credit, he doesn't stop me or interrupt my process. He just continues to watch. I can't help but notice the smallest movement from his hook as it runs back and forth along the side of his pants. Is he nervous? No, he's probably bored.

Without a word, I pick up my tattoo gun and turn it on, commencing the familiar soothing buzz that reminds me of a swarm of honeybees. Time to do this thing.

The moment the needle hits his chest, Hook's body jerks like he's been electrocuted.

CHAPTER 4

PAIN GIVES ME A CHUBBY

HOOK

"Don't stop," I order when Tink pulls back.

The pressure of the needle feels like a charged lightning bolt, and my heart thumps so hard and fast I'm half surprised it doesn't burst out of my chest. A sheen of sweat instantly breaks out all over my body.

"This isn't normal," she mutters, but does as I say.

A dry half-cough, half-laugh escapes me even as the pain assaults me like a hundred white-hot needles.

The fairy stays the course, outlining the key.

Fae fucking hell, I hope this works. I can't help but pant as if I've run ten miles in two minutes.

"So what kind of curse is this?" Tink asks. She tries to keep her expression blank and indifferent, but the tension around her eyes tells me all I need to know about her. She feels my pain, and she's trying to distract me from it.

I almost say she doesn't need to bother to entertain me. I'm not a sick child or someone who can't handle their share of pain. Yet, I give in.

"It ensures one of my crewmembers will betray me on every bloody voyage."

"Every voyage?" She lets out a low whistle with exaggerated false concern. "Oh, please. What a sob story. You're a pirate, Hook. Betrayal is practically in your job description."

The needle hits a spot that turns to living fire. My hips shoot off the chair as I grit my teeth at the spike of sensation. A second wave of sweat breaks out across my entire body as my flesh revolts against what I'm putting it through.

A fresh wave of irritation rises, tightening my jaw as I watch her.

"For any voyage to work, the crew must work as a cohesive unit. I may not be the world's nicest guy, but I pride myself on running a tight ship." My tone comes out harsh.

My brain catches up before I've even finished biting out the words.

If I scare her off, I will be royally fucked.

But Tink doesn't recoil or pause her ministrations. She simply quirks her lips to the side, eyes focused on my chest. "I guess that makes sense," she says impassively. "What happened on your last voyage?"

She's still trying to distract me from the pain. Ridiculous chit.

As Tink leans over to examine my tattoo, her wings catch my eye, their iridescent surface shimmering under the bright shop lights. The delicate structures are mesmerizing, almost translucent, with intricate veins running through them. I wonder how they would feel under my fingertips—smooth and cool, or warm and thrumming with her magic?

"Also, if you fuck up my chair with that hook of yours,

I'll kick your ass." She says it so deadpan an actual laugh escapes me. Emerald eyes fly up to meet mine with open surprise.

I'd love to see her try. I could subdue this little blonde pixie in a matter of moments, but I have a feeling she'd put up a good fight. I'd guess her to be a scrappy fighter. She'd use teeth and nails and any other dirty means of winning.

My cock twitches at the thought.

My dirty little pixie.

Oh, I like that far too much. My mind tumbles into another kind of fight. One where I've stripped her glowing, sun-kissed skin bare, and she fights me for dominance as we fuck against every surface in this place.

"Pain gives you a chubby, huh?" she asks in that flat tone again. "Can't say I'm surprised."

My laugh comes out as a breathless husk, another spike of pain hitting me at the same time as her words.

"What can I say? A little pain paired with pleasure is the best way to live." I don't apologize or bother to cover my rising mast.

After swallowing over a particularly hot spot, I decide to answer her question.

"During the last voyage, my first mate turned on me. He tried to sell me out to the authorities, setting us up for a rendezvous that turned out to be a trap." My voice tightens from a different kind of pain. I'd trained the lad for years, and I molded him from a spoiled upstart with soft hands into a reliable, capable seaman. Erik was the best kind of man and one I'd been proud to call a friend until he turned on me for the chance to captain a ship of his own.

"Did you kill him?" Tink's voice is quiet, almost cautious.

Is she scared of the answer? Is she worried I'll do the same to her?

That bothers me for some reason, which makes me want to put the fear of me in her all the more. Make sure she knows I can't be trusted, that I'm a bad, bad man.

But I need her. I can't push her away.

"No," I sigh in dark defeat. "It wasn't his fault. It was the damn curse."

Another white-hot spark of pain has me gripping the armrest with a death grip. I remain mindful to not rip up the other armrest with my hook, though I'd love nothing better than to sink it into the soft leather.

"Did you get arrested then?" Tink bites down on the corner of her lip as she concentrates on replicating the key. Between that expression and her thick black glasses, I find myself completely captivated by her. I know that intensity. It's the focus and flow of one doing something that is their calling. It's something vital down to the bones. I know it all too well.

I enter that flow every time I set foot on the *Jolly Roger* and take to the seas. There is nothing else like it.

Some people never find their purpose, and I pity them.

"No, I managed to escape, but a lot of good hands died that day." Something bitter seeps into my mouth.

"And the first mate?"

"He has his own ship now," I say, unsure which stings more, her words or what she's doing. "*Captain* Erik made out with his spoils despite this old pirate slipping away yet again."

"So if you know you will always be betrayed, why do you keep sailing?"

"Why do you do what you do?"

Tink looks up at that, the needle hovering above my

chest. Suddenly I'm drowning in the twin jewels of her eyes.

"Because I must." Her lips barely move as she murmurs the words.

I nod in solidarity, my heart pounding against my ribs with more insistence than a moment ago. "Because I must."

The key slowly but surely takes form over the curse. Thankfully, the pain remains somewhat constant.

"Did you get these because of that mermaid you killed?" Tink's voice is tight.

"Do you always ask this many questions?" I'm done playing Mr. Nice Pirate. The pain is making me cranky and impatient. It took fifteen years to find this key, and now that I'm so close to being freed from one of my curses, I'm sitting on pins and needles to see if it will work.

Or rather, getting jabbed repeatedly by a needle of horrendous pain and torment.

I don't want to fucking talk about my past. I don't want to talk to her.

Mainly because I do.

Tink shrugs, unfazed by my harshness yet again. We fall into a silence that is only broken by my occasional grunt or groan of pain.

"Almost done," Tink announces after what feels like an eternity.

As the last line of detail is completed, a crack of silent thunder detonates in the parlor.

All the atoms of my being split with fervor. My chest feels like it cracks open with the force exploding from the curse. I grip the armrest as I jerk up, crying out in raw agony.

I don't know how long it takes before the energy calms in and around me. When I look down, I find the mark entirely erased from my chest. Instead, there are only the tattoos I got in my youth that have been covered this whole time. Treasure and mermaid tails all twining around the anchor on my heart.

How fucking ironic.

Before I'm aware of the room or my body, I'm on my feet. Power still pulses in the room and it has me hard as a rock.

Blood rushes with hot insistence, throbbing all through my dick and booming in my ears. Energy crackles through my body, and I'm desperate, mindless with the need to burn it off.

I meet the pixie's gaze, and her pupils are blown into black pits. Her wings flap in quick little spurts, gold dust wafting off them.

Pixie dust.

Whatever has me in its thrall is also affecting her. Her small pert breasts heave, and she grips the counter behind her as if it will keep her grounded. My attention fixates on that small jewel nestled in her belly button. My tongue aches to dip into her navel, to feel the metal against my lips.

I want her. I want her more than anything I've ever wanted in my entire existence. There is no use fighting it. Pirates take what they want.

I grab her roughly, crushing my lips to hers in a frenzied kiss.

CHAPTER 5
FUCK ME DIRTY
TINK

A pirate plunders. And that's exactly what Captain James T. Hook is doing—devouring me with every kiss. He doesn't kiss. He takes.

And I meet him with the frenzy of my own greedy fervor.

Must fuck, must rut, must come.

A tidal wave of lust and need crashes over me the moment the curse shatters. It's a physical force that wipes out all coherent thought. I'm drowning in it, aching, empty.

The urge to have him filling me, possessing me, over-rides everything else—even the hatred simmering between us. All I can think about is riding his hot, hard cock until I'm screaming my release.

Somewhere in the back of my mind, I know that breaking the curse has unleashed this uncontrollable force. A lust bomb more potent than my pixie dust. But the rest of me doesn't give a single solitary witchtit.

The salty taste of him, the curve of his lips—it's intoxicating. I'm drowning in a man I should despise, a man more despicable than the filthiest muck on earth.

And I want him to fuck me dirty.

Hook backs me against the counter, and my legs spread instinctively. His height dwarfs mine, forcing him to crouch to claim my mouth again and again.

Thunder cracks outside, followed by a rolling kaboom that rattles all the instruments in my shop.

My hands roam over his heated muscles, frustrated by the barrier of these damn latex gloves. His tongue sweeps into my mouth. When I try to fight for dominance, he nips my lips, bending me backward until I submit.

I can't fight it. I'm so empty. My inner muscles clench, needing to be filled. I need friction, I need to be penetrated, to be dicked down until there's nothing left of me.

The scratchy sound of fabric tearing reaches my ears before I realize he caught his hook on my shirt. He rips away the fabric without pause or shame.

A small part of me protests, but I want him so badly I can't bring myself to speak. All I can do is moan wantonly as the chill of his hook slides along my hot, sensitive flesh.

I have to get these clothes off. I need his bare skin against mine.

The moment my lavender lace bra is exposed, he cuts it away with savage force.

"Fae fucking hell." He says the curse like a prayer. "Look at these precious little titties." He latches on and suckles first one, then the other. Shocks of pleasure zip through me as he rolls my nipples between his teeth and tongue. It only drives my need higher until my panties are soaked.

When his hook scrapes my nipple, a jolt of electricity shoots straight to my core.

"Fuck," I hiss as the metal grazes me. "We should stop." My words are half swallowed up by his kisses.

"I can't," he rasps, voice rough and raw. His need

mirrors mine, a desperate, consuming hunger. "I'm going to fuck you so hard, you won't know your own name," he murmurs, voice filled with dark amusement.

Time and space slip away. Everything blurs together. There is only the hot hard muscle and strong, calloused hand of Hook, the unrelenting suction of his scalding mouth on my tits.

His boots and pants hit the wall with a crash. My shorts and strappy wedges disappear along with my panties, which do their best to cling to my wet center. Hook lets out a satisfied groan as he peels them away from me.

This is the point where some men rear back in shock or surprise.

Hook's expression darkens with hunger as he spreads me open, his eyes locked on the glint of my piercings. The cool metal sends a shiver through me, anticipation thrumming in my veins, each ring catching the light and amplifying the feeling.

"So wet. Look how perfect your juicy little pierced cunt is."

Hook's language is shocking. Crass. Totally...making me wetter.

"Keep them on," he barks when I reach to remove my glasses. "I'm going to fuck you with them on. Leave the gloves on too."

A hot shiver rakes through me.

His calloused digit slips between my folds. A half-gasp, half-shriek escapes me. Oh, sweet witchtits, it's sooo good.

It's so fucking good, yet I'm desperate for more.

As if knowing exactly what I need, there is no teasing. He pistons in and out of me, before adding a second finger. I grip his shoulders. He's still bent over to even out our height difference.

His hook digs into the counter next to me. I don't even care that he's scoring the surface.

My mouth waters at the sight of his hard length. The large mushroom head is as tan as the rest of him. The vague thought of him walking his ship stark naked crosses my mind. Surely not though...

"Such a wet little cunny on my pierced pixie." He coos the words even as he finger-fucks me higher to where I want to go, to where I need to break.

When he pulls his hand away, I nearly scream in frustration, the loss unbearable.

He tries to turn me around; he wants to fuck me from behind.

I grab the hair at the base of his skull, jerking his head, getting his attention.

"No," I snarl.

We continue to kiss, push, and pull each other. Finally, he backs us into the darkened front room. The outside street is obscured as the storm rages down, pouring violent sheets of water against the glass. We move toward the couch, but we don't make it. I push him, and he falls on his ass. The clink of his hook hitting the tile floor only fuels the fire in me.

I drop on top of him, easily sinking down on his cock.

A bolt lights up the sky, his ocean-blue eyes reflecting the heat as I cry out.

Oh, fae fucks.

It's too much. It's not enough. It's perfect.

Thunder explodes in a bone-shaking kaboom as he penetrates me to the hilt. My head drops back, and pleasure and fullness drive everything else out of my mind. I ride him with abandon, grinding my clit directly on his pelvic bone.

"Fucking hell," he snarls. Then he rolls us. My wings fold instinctively so they aren't crushed when I'm laid out on my back.

Hook grabs my legs and raises them as he gets on his knees to plow into me with a power I've never been the recipient of before. He stretches me past my limits.

Pressure pushes and climbs, my muscles seizing around the intensity. I twist and rise, nearing my climax, but I want Hook to submit to me just a hairsbreadth more.

We are like a couple of animals fighting for the alpha position. He has the benefit of sheer size and strength, but I'm not afraid to bite and claw as we fuck. I nip at his earlobe, tugging on the row of silver hoops with my teeth, reveling in the growl that rumbles through his chest. His skin tastes of salt and something so deliciously masculine, I'm instantly addicted.

"I know you are close to coming, you stubborn little pixie," he growls. "Give it up. Let those legs shake and cream all over my dick, fairy."

"Fuck you," I grit out through my teeth, even as it takes everything to hold my release at bay.

That raspy laugh sends ripples through my pussy. I almost lose control but manage to snatch it back just in time.

"Maybe we should move this to your place?" he suggests glibly. "Things will only get messier from here."

My wings explode open, beating frantically as I push him back. Hook hits his ass for the second time, and I'm on top again. Partly fueled by fear, I claw into his chest.

No. The word resounds in my mind. I would never invite him into my home. Not someone like him. Not after what happened last time.

Instead of answering, I use his body to chase my own pleasure.

With a few quick thrusts of my hips, I find the perfect angle. I shatter into incoherent screams, scraping my blunt nails over his washboard abs as I convulse, twitch, and come like I've never come before in my life.

Hot, blinding static washes away my vision as pleasure-fueled earthquakes rock me from sense and shoot me up into outer space.

A thumb finds my clit, and the pirate captain rubs my nub with the expertise of my own fingers on a Friday night after a bottle of rosé and a Henry Cavill movie marathon.

He drags my orgasm out until I'm gasping for breath and quaking like an aspen leaf in a hurricane.

Then he lets out a hoarse shout as his hips slam into mine once, twice, and then stall out. Warmth floods me, fuzzing up the back of my brain.

I should calm down.

I should question what the hell just happened.

I should ask if he's had the birth control shot. I haven't heard of him leaving behind a trail of bastards in his travels, but I should be careful.

But the tingles of magic energy still sizzle through me, clouding my mind. Power and magic wash away all thoughts of caution.

More. Need more.

"Greedy little slut, aren't you?" Hook lets out that raspy chuckle again.

I realize I voiced my need out loud, but he's just as affected. Hook's blue eyes are a raging storm of want that mirrors my own.

"I'll give you what you need," he purrs.

CHAPTER 6
SHIVER ME TIMBERS
HOOK

The force unleashed by the shattered curse surges through my bloodstream. It obliterates any rational thought, leaving only an intense desire to claim the fairy in front of me.

"I *take* what I want," Tink growls in response to my claim that I'll give her what she needs. Her defiance only stokes the flames of my desire.

Something swells inside me. Respect.

She's a survivor, just like me. I can see it in the way she holds herself, the way she refuses to back down even in the face of a notorious pirate captain. This pixie has fought tooth and nail for everything she has, and she's not afraid to keep fighting for what she wants.

I know that hunger, that desperate need to seize any scrap of happiness or pleasure in a world that's only ever tried to beat you down. When you've had everything ripped away from you, time and time again, you learn the only way to get what you want is to take it for yourself.

And right now, I want her. I want to ruin her.

I pull out of her tight heat, smirking at the needy

whimper that escapes her kiss-swollen lips. My cock throbs, still hard as steel, ready to plunder her sweet quim and claim her again.

If one could bottle up the essence of this curse, they'd make an easy million. Not that I need much time to rise to the occasion again, but this? This is beyond natural.

With one hand, I lift her ass. I relish the way her wings flutter, catching air until she's perched on the edge of the checkout counter. I push her thighs apart, knowing the stinging effect of my cold metal hook shocks her feverish skin. When I slide it up her slit, her eyes fly wide open, pupils blown with lust and a hint of fear.

"Such a wet little fairy," I rasp, drinking in the dark desire on her face. "That cunny wants me to fuck it again, doesn't it?"

Tink flushes, a fresh gush of arousal coating my hook, but the haughty set of her jaw remains. I'll enjoy breaking her of that willful pride.

Leaning in, I scrape my teeth on the shell of her ear. "I'm going to eat the pixie dust right out of your pussy." Then, before she can protest, I drop to my knees and latch onto her dripping lower lips.

Tink bucks against my mouth, fingers tangling in my hair as I feast on her sweet nectar. I don't care that my seed is still inside her, marking her as mine—I'll lick every trace of it from her quivering cunt then fill her with more.

My tongue traces the delicate folds of her sex, the metal of her piercings a thrilling contrast.

Sliding two fingers into her tight channel, I pump mercilessly, reveling in the broken sounds spilling from her lips. My fingers rub along her piercings with each thrust, eliciting a sharp gasp of pleasure from her kiss-swollen lips.

"That's it, my little cumslut," I growl into her clit. "You

like being a filthy pixie, letting me lick you up. You taste like peaches drenched in my sex. I bet none of the moronic boys you fuck can make you feel like this, can they? They don't know how to crack you open, to find all those sweet spots that make you scream."

I can't help but wonder how many inexperienced boys have had her like this, their clumsy touches and fumbling caresses failing to unlock the true depths of her pleasure. They probably only saw her as this edgy little thing, failing to appreciate the true strength underneath. The animal that claws and bites, bucks and fights as she fucks. A fighter at her core.

Still, I taste the innocence beneath the bravado, the untapped well of desire waiting to be unleashed by a man who knows how to exploit every hidden trigger, every secret button.

Her thighs tremble, her back arching as my words send shudders through her slight frame. I curl my fingers, stroking that sensitive spot inside her. My skilled touch, honed by years of experience, has her writhing beneath me, desperate for more. Just where I want her.

I'm not the jealous type. Hell, I'm not the committing type. But I need her to know that none of the idiots she's fucked before could satisfy her. That she deserves more.

You? a skeptical voice asks in my head.

I brush the thought away and tap my tongue against her clit with quick, violent lashes until my jaw aches and her nails dig painfully into my scalp.

But it's not enough. I need to be back inside her, splitting her open on my aching cock.

Not yet. Not until you get what you want from her first.

"I'm going to make you come so hard, you'll forget every fumbling touch, every disappointing fuck you've ever had. You'll spill like an ocean wave drenching the sand, and you'll know that only a real man can give you what you need."

Tink's eyes snap open, glaring down at me with fury and raw hunger. "Shut up and fu—" Her words cut off into a strangled moan as I tap my tongue against her clit, quick and precise. She claws at my scalp. Her body tightens around my fingers as she screams her pleasure for all the world to hear.

But I'm not done with her yet.

Before her climax fades, I surge to my feet, driving back into her. She's so tight, so perfect around me, like she was made for me.

"You're mine, pixie," I snarl against her throat, punctuating my words with sharp, deep thrusts. "This sweet cunt belongs to me now. I'm going to ruin you for anyone else. Do you understand me?"

Tink rakes her nails down my back in response, the sting only spurring me on. "Fuck you, pirate," she pants, even as she rocks her hips to meet my brutal pace. "I hate you."

"Keep telling yourself that, fairy," I rasp, catching her nipple between my teeth. "Your body knows the truth. No boy could ever make you feel the things I can. You'll never be satisfied with anyone after me, not after you've had a taste of what a real man can do to you."

I'll make sure she never forgets it. I'll fuck her on every surface of this shop, claim her so thoroughly she'll never be able to think of anything but my cock buried inside her, my hands on her skin, my mouth devouring her.

And I'll prove it to her, over and over again, until she's ruined for anyone else. Until the only thing she craves is the touch of a real man—the touch of a pirate king.

I flip Tink over the counter as I drive into her from behind. She pushes back, matching my brutal pace, her heat gripping me like a velvet fist. The sight of her wings quivering with every impact, the sound of her breathless moans filling the air—it's enough to push me to the brink.

Unable to resist any longer, I trace my fingers along the delicate edge of her wing. Tink gasps. The chitin is surprisingly warm to the touch, thrumming with life and magic. A wave of protectiveness crashes over me, but I shove it down.

"How you take my cock like a wanton little slut," I growl, my hook scraping the counter as I lean over her, pressing her into the unyielding surface. "Looks like you belong in the dirt with me. Let go of that false pride and admit it. You crave this."

Tink snarls beneath me, her back arching as she tries to throw me off. But her body responds, the telltale flutter of her walls against my shaft betraying her true desires.

"Fuck you," she spits, even as she grinds, seeking more of the friction she craves. "I'm nothing like you."

I laugh darkly as I circle her clit with deft fingers. "Keep telling yourself that, love. But looks like deep down, you're just as filthy as I am, just as hungry for the depravity only I can give you."

Magic pulses around us, through us, amplifying every sensation until it's almost too much to bear. Tink's head falls forward, her fingers scrabbling for purchase on the smooth countertop as I pound into her, chasing the release that hovers just out of reach.

"Come for me, fairy. Let that sweet cunt milk my cock."

Tink's head falls forward, her body tensing as she clenches me like a vise. "F-fuck," she sobs, her release triggering my own.

I bury myself to the hilt, emptying every last drop inside as I grind against her ass. The primal urge to claim her, to make her mine, surges through me, even as my rational mind rejects the notion.

I don't do commitment, don't tie myself to anyone or anything beyond the call of the sea and the promise of the next plunder. From the time I was a child, I knew there was no one and nothing I would weigh anchor for. Not for long anyway.

And yet, as Tinkerbell pulses around me, her shape molding so perfectly to mine, a traitorous part of me whispers that she could be the greatest treasure of all.

Even as the aftershocks fade, my desire renews. My cock twitches inside her still-fluttering walls. The curse's magic is unrelenting, and I can see the same bottomless pit of need reflected in Tink's half-lidded eyes.

"We're far from done, fairy," I rasp, pulling out only to flip her, mindful of her delicate wings. "I'm going to fuck you until all you know is my cock splitting you open."

Tink's eyes blaze with fury and desperation, her hands fisting in my hair as she drags me into a brutal kiss. "Then shut up and do it," she hisses into my lips. "Fuck me like you hate me, pirate."

And I do, driving into her with punishing force, the wet sound of our joining bodies obscene in the charged air. Tink meets me thrust for thrust. Her nails raking bloody furrows down my back, urging me on. We're lost to the same all-consuming hunger.

Magic throbs around and through us, blurring the lines between pain and pleasure, hate and desire. We've fucked each other into oblivion, but still, it's not enough.

A small part of me is terrified I may never get enough of her.

CHAPTER 7
A PARTING KISS
HOOK

Blinking my eyes open, my back screams in pain from being laid out against a cold, hard tile floor. Suddenly, I feel my age all too well. I start to stretch my arms overhead but halt the motion when I find myself trapped under a tiny, warm body.

Tink.

One of us grabbed the knit blanket from the loveseat, though I don't remember who. Her breathing is heavy, and her makeup is smudged badly. Black eyeshadow and the ghost of her pink lipstick are smeared all over her face.

Blame the pirate in me, but I like her dirty, roughed up, and full of my cum. Even now, my dick twitches, though it lacks the manic, magic-fueled energy that possessed it before.

At some point, the magic ebbed enough for her to demand rather sensibly that I confess if I'm riddled with STDs from being a man slut on the seven seas.

While I fully intend to put that title on a business card later, I made sure to reassure her that I prioritize my health as much as running my ship efficiently.

I've received the birth control shot and am clear of disease. It seemed enough to appease her. She assured me she was in the same boat though I didn't ask. I don't think my dick would have changed course even if she'd told me otherwise.

We passed out after five hours of aggressive, uncontrollable fucking. With a glance at the wall clock, I note there's about an hour left before sunrise.

A groan escapes Tink as she shifts. Even in the dark, her green eyes are luminous as she blinks them open sleepily. "What the fae fucks happened?" Exhaustion and excessive screaming have roughened her normally melodic voice. Her elegant fingers try to swipe the makeup from under her eyes.

"You did your job a little too well."

She grabs the blanket, covering up those perfect little pink tits. "Fuck you. This isn't my fault. I had no intention of—"

I roll her onto her back. The tip of my hook scrapes along her jugular, silencing her. Tink swallows hard, and I follow the movement. This close to her sparkling golden skin, I'm tempted to lick her from brow to pussy all over again.

"I didn't say it was your fault, pixie," I say in a low, even voice. "You did what I asked. Neither of us knew what the consequences would be. And for that..." I trail off, caught in awe of her again.

Tink glares at me, fingers still tightly curled into the blanket over her chest. Defiance radiates from her features, and I'm filled with satisfaction at pinning her down.

But then it's not enough to have her at my mercy. A literal weight has been lifted from my chest. The curse is gone.

"I thank you." As I pull my hook away, I lean down until my lips are a hairsbreadth from hers.

I give her one beat. Two.

More than enough time to push me off. To tell me no.

Her little shuddering inhale tells me all I need to know.

I kiss her slowly, taking my time to explore the sweetness of her. I can't help but push in deeper and taste more, with a passionate intensity I don't ever remember extending to anyone before. At this moment, I am not the pirate who takes without remorse—I am a willing servant to her pleasure, to give her all I have in thanks.

She lets out a little whimper into my mouth, and fuck if I'm not hardening against the silken skin of her stomach despite being raw and sore beyond measure.

While my hand tangles its way into her mass of hair, I stroke the cold curve of my hook down her jawline, then run it down her arm until gooseflesh erupts in its wake.

The softness of her skin, the soft resistance of her lips—it's intoxicating. But just as quickly as the passion flares, reality crashes in.

When I draw back, her eyes blaze with defiance and something darker, something complicated.

"Don't think this changes anything," she says finally, her voice steady but edged with lingering anger. "You may be free of one curse, but you're still the same pirate scum who preys on my kind."

A grin tugs at my lips, more out of habit than humor. "And you're still the uppity little pixie who thinks she's better than everyone else." The words come out harsher than I intend, but there's truth in them.

We stare at each other, the weight of what happened and what remains unsaid pressing down on us. The connection between us is undeniable, yet it does nothing to bridge the chasm of animosity that still exists.

Then I get up, not bothering to cover up my nude form.

"I'll be back," I say, the words a promise and a threat. "There are still two curses left."

Her jaw tightens, wrapping the blanket more tightly around herself as she sits up.

She doesn't confirm that she'll help me, but she doesn't warn me off coming back either.

As I gather my discarded clothes and head for the door, I can't resist casting a final glance back. She holds onto the checkout counter as if it's the only thing holding her up. Her eyes meet mine, stormy emotions swirling in their depths.

The insanity of the curse breaking has passed, but the overwhelming need to close the space between us and kiss her yet again grips me.

Which is what has me out the door faster than a shot, walking at a clip like the devil is nipping at my heels.

This pirate doesn't drop anchor for anyone, and I'll be damned if I start getting notions over a green-eyed little upstart even if she fucks like an animal and comes so very pretty-like.

I'd only destroy her like I do everything else.

CHAPTER 8

CAPTURE THE KEY

HOOK

12 months later

The storm rages around me, rain lashing the deck of the *Jolly Roger*. The ship cuts through the waves with practiced precision, a testament to my skill and my crew's loyalty.

Lightning flashes, illuminating the scene before me: Marcus Kane, bound and kneeling, drenched to the bone. His greasy hair hangs in his face, and his mouth twists into a defiant sneer, even now. The man reeks of desperation. Fear and sour sweat cuts through the cold, salty air.

Kane is a wretched excuse for a man. His hands have trafficked in the darkest deals—selling children to slavers, poisoning wells for profit, and betraying anyone foolish enough to trust him. His list of sins could wrap around the length of my ship, and I have no qualms about adding to his tally of pain.

The crew watches silently, their faces hard and unreadable, trusting me to handle this final reckoning. The storm's fury reflects my own, an unrelenting force that won't be deterred. Kane's ship, stripped and helpless, rocks nearby, a symbol of his impotence.

I stride forward, each step deliberate, the weight of the key around his neck drawing my gaze.

Kane coughs, spitting blood onto the deck. "You think you're better than me, Hook?" he snarls, voice rough and bitter. "You're just another scumbag pirate."

I kneel in front of him, my face inches from his, the cold metal of my hook pressing lightly into his neck. His eyes, bloodshot and wild, stare back at me. There's a flicker of fear there, poorly masked by his bravado. The key glints in the flickering light, a small piece of metal holding so much power over me.

"The difference," I say, my quiet voice cutting through the wind and rain, "is that I don't pretend to be something I'm not." With a swift motion, I drag my hook across his throat. The cut is clean and precise. Blood sprays, hot and dark against the cold air, mingling with the rain as Kane's life spills out of him.

The gurgle that escapes his lips is brief. His eyes go wide with shock, then dull as the last vestiges of life leave his body. The metallic scent of blood intermingles with the briny sea air, a potent reminder of the life taken. The storm seems to rage harder for a moment, as if protesting this final act.

I unfasten the key from around Kane's neck, feeling its weight in my hand. It's cold, slick with blood and rain. The small, ornate object is the key to breaking another of my curses and holding it feels like reclaiming a piece of my freedom. The *Jolly Roger* sways beneath my feet, steady and sure even in the chaos of the storm, a testament to my mastery of the seas.

As the crew moves to dispose of Kane's body, I stand

tall, the storm a wild dance around me. The lightning casts a brief, harsh light on the scene—Kane's limp form, the dark, churning waves, and the grim determination on the faces of my men. My ship, my crew, and my reputation as the best damn pirate to sail these seas—all of it holds strong, even as nature itself tries to break us.

I walk to the edge of the deck, the wind whipping my coat, and look out at the storm-tossed horizon. The curse that ensured betrayal on every voyage is finally lifted. For the first time in years, the constant, gnawing fear and anticipation is absent. The trust I've placed in my crew, and they in me, can finally stand unchallenged by the mermaid's dark magic.

Yet, even as I revel in this victory, my thoughts turn to Tink. Nearly a year has passed since I last saw her, since she removed the first curse. The memory of her sharp tongue and fierce eyes lingers, along with the echo of the explosive energy between us.

As the rain beats down, I wonder if that same energy will flare when we meet again. Will she help me, especially after what happened the last time?

The key in my hand is cold, but the thought of her ignites a warmth deep in my chest. A year is a long time, but I haven't forgotten a single detail about her. Not the flecks of gold in her brilliant turquoise-emerald eyes that turn to liquid fire when she's irate. Not the honeyed floral taste of her perfect sun-kissed skin. Not the taste of her perfect little cunt. My tongue strains with the need to swipe up to those perfect tight folds until they loosen and cream for me.

She's a little upstart who sits on her throne of pride and judgment, but fuck if I haven't thought of a million more ways to corrupt and degrade her until she's on my level again. I want to drag her into the muck with me. But only because I know she likes it so much.

Fae fucks, man. Get it out of your head. If you want her help again, you can't lead with wanting to fuck her dirty. She'll put you out on your ass faster than you can say shiver me timbers.

I turn back to the crew, issuing commands to prepare for our next journey. The storm may rage, but the *Jolly Roger* and her captain are undaunted. I have a mission, a path set before me, and no storm or curse will stand in my way. The horizon stretches out, full of danger and promise, and somewhere beyond it, Tink awaits.

With the taste of salt on my lips and the burn of antici-pation in my chest, I know it's time to head to land.

CHAPTER 9
A PIRATE'S PLEA
TINK

I curse myself for not locking the door when I hear the happy tinkle of the welcome bell.

My wings flap with agitation. Two clients bailed on me, I burned myself with hot tea, and my unreliable internet delayed payments. The process took so long that sweat formed at the back of my neck as my client tapped their foot. I can already tell I'm getting a bad review, a cherry on top of the one that already appeared online this morning.

0/5 stars. Don't go to Inked by Tink for one of her so-called magic markings. She gave me a tattoo of a raccoon in a trash can. The only one who is trash here is the tattoo artist.

I tried to explain at the time, my tattoos are infused with magic. If you choose the pixie special, you get the tattoo you are supposed to have.

It's not like I understand the cosmic significance of why the magic deigned she be branded with a trash panda. But one look at the design and her face fell harder than an anvil. It's not what she wanted to see branded on her body forever.

My magic messages are never wrong, but it sucks when clients aren't receptive. Maybe one day she'll understand what the message is for, but I doubt I'll ever get the end of that story.

Pushing aside the current of ire, I storm out into the front room where the floor is already slickened from the torrential rain outside being let in from the open front door.

"I'm closed—"

I stop in my tracks. My heart flies up, lodging itself in my throat.

It's him.

Soaked from the raging storm outside, he audibly drips into the puddle now on my tile floor with little *tik-tik-tiks*.

It's been a year. A year since I unlocked Captain Hook's curse, and we fucked each other into oblivion.

I'd like to say I didn't think of him again after he left. But even after the soreness between my legs abated a full week later, the pirate never strayed far from my mind.

Dark eyes flash at me through long black, curly hair. The corner of his lips quirk upward in a way I've come to know too well—a smile or a sneer, I'll likely never know for sure.

At least a week's worth of stubble covers his sun-darkened face. His sleeves are pushed up, the tendons in his forearms shifting as he balls his hand into a fist before releasing. Though his other hand is a literal hook, the forearm tenses on that side as well.

It takes a lot of raw power to run a ship the way he does.

My eyes drink him in, taking in a new element that wasn't there before. An angry red scar that slashes across his throat. Someone tried to kill Hook and by the looks of it, they must have gotten close.

"Hiya, Tink." Has my name ever passed his lips before? And if it did, did I like it this much?

His voice is raspy and sends shivers rattling up and down my spine before landing hotly in my lower belly. It's even rougher than before. Is that from having his jugular slit?

I open my mouth to ask what he's doing here, but I already know. He found the second key. He wants me to break the second curse.

As if reading my mind, he pulls out the tattered cloth, concealing the object wrapped inside. There's hesitation. A question on his face.

"No," I snap, feeling my irritation rise. "I'm not helping you again."

A wad of cash materializes in his fist, even bigger than the last time, but I barrel on. "And I'm sure as hell not going to let you waltz in here, drop some money on the counter, expecting me to ink you up and fuck again."

The words taste bitter in my mouth, but I force them out, holding onto my resolve. The memory of our last encounter flashes through my mind, and my body betrays me with a heated flush.

Damn it, Tink, get a grip.

His fingers tighten around the thick folds of bills before he slips them back into his pocket.

"Then what do you want?" he asks quietly, his voice rougher, more sincere. "Whatever it is, I'll get it for you."

"What could you possibly offer me that would make me want to go through that again?" I retort, narrowing my eyes.

His eyes flash with dark promise. "What does your heart desire? I swear I'll get it for you. Anything."

Anything.

I could laugh.

"What I want..." I inhale deeply through my nose, trying to control my emotions, "you can't give me."

Death takes and it doesn't give back. Not even to a damned pirate captain.

Hook's jaw tightens, and for a moment, I think he's going to lash out or throw some smart-ass remark back at me. But instead, he just looks defeated. Something in my chest pinches, and I don't like it.

"Go to someone else." I do my best to keep my tone cold, but my fuck off vibes are wavering in the wake of his pitiful blue stare. "There are other tattoo artists out there, other magical ones, remember? You don't need me." I cross my arms in finality. The last part is said with bitter resentment.

Because I don't like the idea of someone else being better than me?

Or because I hate the idea he'll end up fucking someone else into oblivion?

If he does, I hope it's an ogre. A literal ogre.

"I lied. There's no one else, Tink." The vulnerability in his voice catches me off guard. "You're the only one who can help me. On this earth, in any realm. It's only you who has the power to break these godsdamn curses."

I shake my head, trying to ignore the ache in my chest at his words. "And why should I care? You steal, you kill, you hurt my kind. Why should I help you? Why should I make your life easier?"

"You think I'm asking for your help because I want an easy life? I've never known an easy day in my entire exis-tence," he snaps back. "These curses—they're not going to kill me, but they make every day a living hell. The sea is the only thing I love, and it's torturing me. It's like loving something with your whole heart and soul and having it reject you, hurt you, every single day."

His words hit me like a punch to the gut, and I struggle to keep my composure. I know that feeling all too well, and the pain of it is raw, real. My heart clenches, but I force myself to stay strong, to keep the walls up around my emotions.

"Please, Tink," he murmurs, his voice low, almost broken. "I need you. I'll do whatever it takes."

I close my eyes, blocking out the pleading in his tone, the raw emotion in his eyes. He's a pirate, a criminal, and I should hate him for what he's done, for what he represents. But the truth is, I don't hate him. And that scares me more than anything else.

"Why should I?" I whisper, hoping against hope he won't come up with a good enough answer.

He hesitates, then steps closer, close enough that I can feel the warmth of his body despite the chill of the rainwater still clinging to him. "Because I have no one else." His voice is barely more than a whisper. "You're the best. You're the only one who can help me."

The sincerity, the way he's laid himself bare in front of me, shakes something loose inside me. I know I shouldn't help him.

"Even if I agree," I say, my resolve weakening, "how do I know this won't end like last time?"

"We'll resist it." His voice is firm. "*I'll* fight it," he adds with more conviction.

I stare at him, my heart hammering in my chest. The magnetic force that brought us together the first time is a stronger pull than ever. The thought of going through that again, of losing control, terrifies me. But the thought of turning him away, of letting him walk out that door and never seeing him again, is even worse.

"Alright," I say finally, my voice trembling. "Let's do it."

CHAPTER 10

STORMY SKIES & SIDE EFFECTS

TINK

Relief washes over Hook's face when I agree to the deal, but there's something else there too—something raw and unguarded that tugs at the edges of my heart.

"Thank you," he murmurs, the words heavy with meaning.

"But there will be absolutely no sex." I stick a finger in his face.

"No sex," he confirms. Even as he says it though, his gaze darkens as if remembering the last time.

"And it's quadruple my price." My voice squeaks.

Thatta girl. You really showed him.

Hook nods, a small smile tilting the corner of his lips.

"Lock the door," I say softly, after swallowing my heart back down in my chest.

He does as I say, flicking off the neon "open" sign as well.

After a year of practice and prep, I still failed at saying no to the one man I should deny.

Worst yet, I'm still not sure if he bested me through my

vanity or empathy, but I make a note to rid myself of both ASAP.

The pirate captain pulls his shirt over his head and drops it on a seat in the corner. His abs clench and ripple as he stretches.

My body instantly responds, dampening at the apex of my thighs. My inner muscles clamp down with memory and need.

"I'll be right with you." Then I shoot out of there and to the bathroom in the back as if a fire has been set on my ass.

Gripping the cold porcelain of the sink, I scrunch up my shoulders before releasing the tension.

"Pull it together, Tink. You've got this and you *will not* fuck the bad pirate again."

The girl in the mirror is losing her shit and needs to get it together. So I take my sweet time retying the handkerchief up around my thick, wavy platinum hair.

Touching up the smoky eye makeup and reapplying my pink lip gloss has nothing to do with the man currently waiting in my seat. It's armor. Just like the tattoos that wrap around my arms and visible skin in intricate, beautiful designs. Just like the many piercings dotting my skin. My primping has everything to do with putting myself together so I can be professional about this.

So he can pull you apart.

I wave the thought away, though I'm more than wet and ready.

Nope, we agreed no matter what happens, we won't be banging again.

You also hate him! He's a bad man. He kills fae like you and steals their treasures. He'd kill you and steal from you too if he didn't need you alive and willing to help. Don't be fooled.

The way he spoke of loving something that didn't love

him back speared me to the wall. I was a cooked goose whether he knew it or not.

I loved some*one*, not some*thing*, that couldn't love me back. It's a pain I wouldn't wish on my worst enemy. Not even Captain James T. Hook.

My blood can run hot, my heart is allowed to pound against my chest, and my lady bits can even get melty, but I need a steady hand for our arrangement.

Going back out there, I walk tall with a sway in my hips, reminding myself I own this place and Hook is in my domain.

Who cares if we fucked like the world was ending?

I close the door behind me without looking at him. I do my best to avoid his gaze, though it bores into me.

Opening a drawer, I pinch out a couple of powder blue gloves, pulling them on. Then I grab the thick, black-rimmed glasses off my shirt and settle them on my face, pushing them up with the palm of my hand.

Every time I put them on, I can't help but remember how Hook ordered me to keep them on after I took off everything else. I have to suppress yet another hot shiver that threatens to rattle me.

Hook is quiet, but the hot waves prickling over my skin let me know he's studying me. I should have left the door open so I wouldn't be trapped in such a small space with him.

I roll over on my wheeled stool and open a waiting hand.

When he doesn't move, I finally lift my gaze to meet his. Hook continues to stare unerringly at me. I don't know what to make of his intense expression. There is an assessment sparking in his eyes that causes a flash of annoyance to spark in me.

"Well?" I ask impatiently. "Don't tell me you didn't find the second key. Otherwise, why would you be here?" My heart does a little skip at the thought he might be here for another reason.

He pulls that little scrap of fabric out again and hands it over. The second key.

With some adjustments, we have the chair situated so he can turn around and expose his back to me.

There are two large designs. One is engraved inside the other yet I can tell they are distinct from one another. It's a massive compass full of clouds and storms. My fingers can't help but trace the lines. The compass moves, the dial slowly looping, ticking forward and backward without rhythm or sense. The clouds in the dial shift and move as if embroiled in a storm they want to unleash.

"Keep that up, pixie, and we won't need an explosive spell to get me hard."

"Shut up," I snap, though it lacks my usual venom toward him. "I'm working."

The Three of Hearts curse ensured a crew member betrayed him on every voyage. Going over the marks I didn't get a good look at last time, I try to remember what the other two curses are for based on the symbols.

Did he even tell me?

Did he fuck the information right out of my brain?

"The clouds promise I will always be met with stormy weather," Hook says as if reading my mind. "I haven't seen a sunny day in sixteen years. It always means treacherous seas. I've lost many a crew member who was tossed overboard into the greedy ocean." His voice is a hypnotic timbre that hits me in my low belly. "The compass means the stars will always betray me. Pirates sail by the stars, but for me, even a clear sky is useless. No matter what, they'd always lead me astray."

"Aren't there instruments you can use to get around?" I unfold the key on my work tray.

He lets out a dry scoff. "Sure, but I can't say I enjoy using them. I miss the stars." Genuine longing tinges his voice as his back rounds further into my touch.

"Do we know which curse this key will unlock?" I ask, turning the key over in my hand. I try to ignore the red splatter covering one side of it.

Blood.

Or maybe tomato juice?

Yeah, he probably spilled his Bloody Mary on the key. Or a dollop of paint?

Wow. The shit I tell myself to justify helping this pirate.

"We do not," Hook says, answering my question.

When I look up, I find Hook twisted around to see my face.

"And do we know if the side effects will be..." *Uncontrollable fucking again?*

I can't bring myself to say it.

He's still staring with that unerring gaze that sticks a hook right in my belly before it pulls. "Unclear. But like I said, I won't touch you. I swear it on my ship's hull."

That's the most sacred item he can swear upon?

"Fantastic." I meant for the word to come out more sarcastic. Then I turn on my tattoo gun, somewhat soothed by the familiar buzz. "Round two it is."

CHAPTER 11

NEVER MAKE A FAIRY CRY

HOOK

Fae fucking bottles on the back of a whale of your mother.

The pain is just as intense as the last time. My fingers dig into the chair while my teeth grit and grind while Tink uses liquid fire on my back.

"No questions today?" I ask after five minutes of silence that presses on me like a literal weight. At least the scent of Tink surrounds me in a comforting little cloud.

She doesn't answer, which infuriates me for some reason.

"No inane chatter or judgment about what a wretched, dirty pirate I am?"

"Is that blood on the key?" she finally asks.

Damn. Of all the questions she could ask, that's what we're going to have to talk about?

"I had to take it from a not-so-nice man when he refused to give it up."

A dry snort comes out of her.

"Believe me, pixie, you think I'm a bad man, you have no idea what kind of scum is out there."

"Right, because you are such a hero when put in the right light."

There she is. My sassy little brat. My hand itches to slap her taut ass.

Suddenly, I crave to see the bare side of her rear turned an angry red from the onslaught of my calloused palm. Something I failed to explore in our previous tryst. I shake off the fantasy.

That will *not* be happening again. I gave her my word.

And I won't break it no matter how tempting she is.

"I may murder and pillage, but I leave the kids out of it. And I don't deal in slaving."

The liquid fire comes to a halt.

I turn to see what holds her up. "Something wrong?" For a moment, the irrational fear hits me that she's out of pixie dust, or maybe she will refuse to help me.

"He sold children?"

She asks the question with such intense concern I instantly want to fold her into my arms. I want to let her know everything is okay.

No. Fuck that.

I need to be glib. I need to put a stop to the sincerity in her voice. I should say something to infuriate her, something personal and insulting.

"Don't worry, pixie. He won't be doing it anymore, not from the bottom of the ocean."

I couldn't bring myself to taunt her, not when she turned so serious. It's not something I take lightly either.

A hiss snakes through my teeth and my back jerks as I'm hit with that razor pain again as she recommences.

"That's fucked up," she says in a hard tone.

"That it is, pixie."

She falls into silence again and heat rises in me. More

agitation. Usually, I hate having to speak to others unless I'm barking commands. But I need to hear her voice.

"Why are you in Boston instead of with all your other little fairy friends?"

"That's none of your business." Her voice is cold, foreboding.

I shouldn't press; I need her to help me. But I can't help myself. "Did they kick you out? Or do you just love the magic-less slums of Boston?"

"This city is my home now." There's a warning in her tone as if I'm about to cross a line disparaging a beloved friend.

But she doesn't belong here. Anyone can see that.

"It's the place you live. But knowing your kind, you deserve to live in some grand oak filled with magic and pixie dust in your fairy realm. Like that tree tattoo you gave that little sick girl."

The tattoo gun turns off with an almost deafening silence.

When I twist this time, I'm surprised to find her face has flushed an almost strawberry red and her eyes brim with glassy, unshed tears.

My stomach jerks and jolts with the realization I stepped on a landmine. Regret rips through me in an instant.

A sensation I usually only equate with the one mistake of my past.

Her glistening pink mouth parts then closes again, like a fish out of water.

"I'm sorry." The words fly out of my mouth before I realize it. I'm not even sure what I'm sorry for, but I am. I'm sorry for whatever it was I said to cause that stricken, heartbroken look on her face.

It shreds my heart like rows of shark teeth.

Her eyes turn unfocused before she clenches them shut, tears spilling down her cheeks. Mascara runs down them in dirty, sad tracks.

"Tink." I turn more fully, grabbing her delicate wrist in mine. My hook digs into my thigh until it pierces my thick slacks. Pain spikes as I dig deeper to break my own skin. I deserve punishment for hurting her. My pixie angel.

She rapidly blinks at me, more tears spilling despite her fight against them.

"Tink, I'm sorry. Don't cry. I can't stand seeing you cry."

"I—" She has to work to find her voice. "You're not wrong." Her words break my heart, and I'm not sure why. My thumb gently caresses the bare delicate bones of her wrist above the glove.

"Turn around," she orders in a steadier voice.

I don't want to obey. I want to force her to tell me what has her so upset. The strange compunction to give her whatever she wants, whatever she needs, overwhelms me. Something I may be feeling for the first time.

I've never felt the need to help anyone else. Not unless it directly or indirectly benefits me.

Still, I release her wrist and turn back around.

The buzz of her tattoo gun kicks up again.

"Tell me," I say, my voice suddenly thick with emotion.

Charged lightning licks my skin once again.

"Okay," she says in a small voice.

CHAPTER 12

THE SUFFERING OF THE SMITTEN

TINK

"You're right. I should be living in a beautiful tree with my people." The words come out, but they feel like razors traveling up my throat.

I use the back of my wrist to wipe away the remaining tears on my cheeks. I hate the hot sting on my face. I hate that I'm so transparent around the absolute last person I should be open with.

"Why aren't you there now?" The pirate asks the question carefully, as if aware he is in dangerous waters.

"Because someone betrayed me, and my home was destroyed." There, better to just say it matter-of-factly.

Hook's back muscles coil and bunch up. "Who?" His voice turns dark, the question full of violent promise.

He doesn't know me. Not really. Sure, we fucked like animals, but that doesn't mean anything. This is a business transaction. Yet I can't help but think he means to avenge me. That if my betrayer's name drops from my lips, Hook will spend his days scouring the earth until he's hunted the offender down and cut him to ribbons.

My stomach churns, unsure if I like the idea or detest it. I can't settle on a decision.

I lick my suddenly dry lips. "He was just a boy. A boy I was terribly in love with."

The muscles under my needle tighten even more.

I press my free hand against his back until he relaxes slightly.

The implied request for more turns the air thick. Hook fills the room with his presence, his unvoiced demand that I go on. He has a power that doesn't come from magic, but it dominates the space around him. It threatens to sweep me away...if I let it.

I don't have to though. I can hold my ground. I've fought hard for my independence, and I will hold onto it with unbreakable determination.

My mouth moves without my brain telling it to. "We both lived in the Wooded Faelands out west."

"Neverland," he says softly.

I nod. "Unlike the perpetually cloudy and rainy west coast, the lush forest of Neverland was almost always bathed in warm sunlight." My skin turns cold as if it misses the sun on that side of the world. It's the same sun that greets me here every day, but it never feels the same.

"We were barely teenagers. He was a little older, and I adored him. He had this air about him, a strength. He could always find the joy and magic in anything. I was smitten." My voice tips up at the end of my confession. His mischievous smile always sent my insides aflutter. I would have done anything he asked, given him my life just to hear him say he treasured me.

I clear my throat, finding it clogged with remnants of the past. "So I did what any smitten teenage girl does. I bared my heart to him. I invited him into my secret home.

Fairies do not let others into their homes often. It's..." I realize I shouldn't be telling Hook all this. He's the last person who should know the secrets of my kind.

"It's where female fairies draw their power, where they nest, and it is a sanctuary unlike any other."

He knows. I want to ask how he knows, but I'm too scared to ask.

"Male fairies don't have this," I explain. Hook probably knows that too, but it will explain why Peter did what he did.

Peter Pan.

His name evokes a shudder that roils with revulsion, regret, and the pain of a wound I know will always remain open and fresh.

"But I brought him inside my home, in the hopes that he would..." I pull back the tattoo gun to blink at the ceiling, noticing a moldy spot. Probably from the storm battering down. I should have someone look at that before I spring a leak or get a real problem.

"In the hopes that he would kiss me." I finish the words quickly, feeling like a stupid little girl. I wanted him to lay his lips on mine so badly. I was fifteen, and he was seventeen. Yet I was sure he saw us as equals, soulmates even.

I brought him inside. My heart pounded, and it was difficult to catch my breath as I waited in anticipation. He strolled around my living quarters, testing the firmness of my rose-colored couch, tracing the antique framed flowers that always brought me joy to look at. When he stopped in front of me, my mind raced, panicked, and jerked around with excitement. Then he leaned in. I closed my eyes, letting my lips pull up ever so slightly, ready to be captured by his gravitational force.

My first kiss, and the only pair of lips I'd know for the

rest of my life because we were destined to be together for all eternity. We'd make magic, fun, and love wherever we went.

A pressure landed on my forehead. I blinked my eyes open in confusion as Peter stuck his hands in his pockets. "It's lovely, Tink. Shall we go out to the lake now?"

I'd been crestfallen.

The moment had been perfect. My treasures and most precious place had been put before his consideration, and he did...nothing with it.

"Idiot boy," Hook sneers, interrupting my recount. I spared him some of the gushier parts of my feelings toward Pan.

A dry, humorless laugh escapes me. "I thought that was the pinnacle of heartbreak." I cried for days. "But then I jumped on the idea he just needed time. We'd end up together forever, so I could afford to wait. It wasn't long after when he put an end to that idea."

Hook shifts under me. Remembering I'm still on the job, I click on the forgotten tool and resume creating the likeness of the second key.

With a hiss, Hook clenches the chair in one hand, making sure his hook stays clear of the leather. I don't love causing him pain, but the action of tattooing allows me to detach from the more painful parts of the story.

"Two weeks later, I came home to find my tree, my home..." I have to hurdle over the grief tearing through me like a thin piece of paper to get the word out. "Dead."

I spotted it from a distance, noting the color of my tree was off from its usual brilliant luminescence of magic and life. My mind couldn't comprehend what I was looking at. Only when I went inside did the horror of the situation begin to dawn on me.

"My home was so beautiful." I choke back the sob threatening to break. I use an elbow to swipe away an errant tear. One would think I'd be able to recount the situation with less emotion; it's not the first time I've had to talk about it. "But then it was this gray, lifeless corpse. It had been drained of all magic. Thankfully, I didn't need to guess why. He was there." My tone darkens. "Waiting for me."

Peter's eyes were red-rimmed, his cheeks gaunt and drawn from stress. As if he even knew what distress was.

Hook jerks under my ministrations. I'd been pressing down too hard. I ease the pressure and try to steady my trembling hand as I hear Peter's voice as if it were yesterday.

"I'm so sorry, Tink. I didn't have a choice."

I have to muscle down the growing lump in my throat.

I couldn't look at him, couldn't bring myself to meet those guilt-ridden eyes. Instead, my gaze fixated on the bark of the tree that had been my home. It used to be a warm, rich brown—the color of freshly turned earth. It always smelled of fresh sap, sweet and comforting, like honey in the spring sunlight.

Now, it reeked of decay. The bark, once glistening with life, had turned dull and brittle. I could still see faint traces of where the once golden sap now oozed in sickly black streaks, like veins of poison. The warm brown had faded to an ashen gray, the vibrancy of life leeched away, leaving only the cold, unyielding grip of death.

I was standing inside the hollow corpse of my friend, my home. The place that had cradled me, protected me, nurtured my magic. Now it was nothing more than a lifeless shell, filled with the stench of rot and betrayal.

"The human girl he really loved, she was dying," I

explain to Hook. "He brought her to my tree, my home, and he used its power to revive her. It drained my home of all magic and killed it forever."

"Tink," Hook rasps.

"So I had to leave my home and make a new one." My words come out hurried as I try to talk over whatever he is going to say. I don't want to hear it. I hate the pity. I've always hated it. It just reminds me of my own stupidity, my naiveté. "I got as far away as I could and carved out a life for myself here in Boston. It may not be the magic faelands I'm from, but it's not so bad. I have friends. I own my business. I help people unlock their potential and use what little magic I have left." My shop, my apartment—they're my fortress, my safe haven where no one can touch me.

It's easy to accrue pixie dust in one's fairy home. It gathers as easily as wiping the sleep from one's eyes. But without my tree, I have to harvest my own pixie dust. It is a painful, painstaking process that involves scraping my wings and destroying my bathroom with the mess. But getting to harness my magic, no matter how painful, to help little girls fight illness, or to support myself off a bad pirate's money, means everything to me.

"Stop," Hook says.

I do what he says, realizing my hand still trembles though the vibrations of my tool have ceased.

He rises from the chair until he's standing, towering over where I sit on my rolling stool. I'm too shaken to get up.

I'll stay right here, thank you very much.

I expect to find that same pity in his eyes. Or maybe he'll openly assess me with the critical gaze of someone who knows they are facing a fool.

Instead, his expression is dark, unreadable.

Hook doesn't say anything for a long moment, just looks at me.

He wants to say something, I just don't know what.

Then he walks by me, opens the door, and disappears into the bathroom across the hall. I let out the breath I've been holding when the door shuts.

My shoulders relax as I'm alone in my space again. The desire to race up to my apartment, my sanctuary, the one place I don't have to put on a brave face crashes into me.

Peeling off my gloves, I cover my face. "Stupid, stupid girl," I berate myself.

Why did I tell him all that? A ruthless, fae-killing pirate.

Because he asked.

CHAPTER 13

ANTAGONIZING THE VILLAIN

HOOK

What is the pixie doing to me?

I stare down the pirate in the mirror, reminding myself that I take care of only one person: me.

So why do I want to find this guy and rip his guts from his insipid body? Acquaint him with all the pain he visited on the blonde fairy with the big green eyes in the next room.

The urge to protect her, to pull her into my arms and kiss away her tears, blazed through me. If it weren't for the liquid fire searing into my back, grounding me, I would have jumped up and done just that.

"Pull it together, Hook. You are here to break free, not shackle yourself to some girl."

Even as I growl the words to myself, my heart thuds against my ribs with insistence, demanding it be heard.

But it won't. I won't fucking listen to the foolish organ.

The sea is my life. Saltwater runs in my veins. The missions I take satisfy me more than any succulent pink mouth ever could. I refuse to give up my freedom for anyone.

Still, the memory of Tink arching her back and crying out in pleasure nearly bowls me over. The way her makeup was smeared over her face when we woke up, and how her head perfectly fit my chest, has burrowed into my brain like a hungry, persistent worm. And her pain... Fae lords help me. It throbs in my chest as if it were my own.

Use her and lose her, Hook.

I repeat the mantra five times before I can bring myself to turn the doorknob and return to the private room where that sweet floral fragrance surrounds me.

Without meeting her gaze, I return to my previous position in the chair, crossing my arms and setting my chin on them.

Tink shuffles with nervous energy, her wings fluttering, filling the air with more of her delicious, intoxicating scent.

"What, no analysis of the situation?" she asks, her insecurity stamped in the question.

Oh, I have an analysis, alright. That no one deserves her consideration, that she is too good for that selfish fucking idiot, that she's too good for this dirty, human city, and that she's far too good for the likes of me. But that doesn't keep me from wanting to take her, capture her, keep her for my own. A treasure I'd never share with anyone.

"Are you almost done?" is what I ask in a clipped tone instead.

She huffs in fury, and when the needle hits my skin, she doesn't hold back. The tattoo gun drives into my flesh with unrelenting fire. A croak escapes my throat, and I swear I hear a satisfied harrumph from her.

"You really aren't as tough as they say." I hear the glower in her tone.

"You don't know a damn thing about me." I grit my teeth as she lances me with particular fury.

"Sure I do. You kill fae creatures for their treasure. Hell, you would probably shake the hand of the guy who ripped the magic from my home. That's what you do, right? Steal magic from others?" Her voice is tight.

My anger rises quick and fast, fueled by the pain she is inflicting.

"You don't know what you're talking about, pixie," I warn.

"I heard about that poor mermaid you tricked. That you seduced her, made her believe she was in love with you until she led you to her treasure, her most prized magical possession. You and Peter should go out for drinks sometime and congratulate each other."

Peter. So that's the idiot fucker's name.

I'm not sure who is running hotter, her or me. The fury in her voice matches what's boiling inside of me. When anger takes hold of me, it becomes a raging storm, and she doesn't want it. She can't handle that.

"You're going to want to shut your mouth, pixie."

"You killed her for it. You selfish son of a bitch." Her volume rises with the accusation. "Everyone knows it. Don't deny it. I recognize the waves on your necklace. The Waves of Poseidon. You took her life and traded it for a protection charm. Though judging by that slash on your neck, it doesn't do all that good of a job."

I remember the way her small, elegant fingers moved my hair and necklaces aside last time. I knew her eyes caught on the blue waves of the magical item.

"And then you murdered her." Tink practically shouts now. "She trusted you, and you killed her so you could take her treasure, you bastard."

The chair goes sprawling as I flip around, backing Tink's rolling chair to the counter before she knows what's happened. My arms cage her in as I lean into her face, my breath ragged and heaving as if I've just run a marathon.

"You don't know what you are fucking talking about."

Instead of cowering from my barely restrained violence, she narrows her eyes at me in a challenging glare. Her gloved hand still holds the tattoo gun while the other is clenched into a fist.

"Oh, you're going to deny you are a murderer now? I thought you loved your bad reputation, intimidating everyone you possibly can?"

Before I can think, my hand grips her by the throat. "I have killed countless scum who deserved to meet their maker at the end of my hook," I hiss into her face. "But I didn't kill her."

Tink's brows twitch and rise in surprise. Then her eyes darken. "Because what? You cared for her?"

I loosen my hold when her words come out breathless, but I don't let go of her dewy, silken throat. The delicate neck bones easily shift under my hand.

"Why?" My smile curves up with all the wickedness of the devil. "Are you jealous, my little pixie?"

Her face becomes a thundercloud. "You're disgusting."

"And yet you enjoy my particular brand of filth." I over enunciate each word, making sure what I say hits her like a hammer. "You're right, I did get close to the mermaid. I coerced her into taking me to the Cave of Wonders. Even though I knew it was protected by an ancient guardian, I still convinced her to take me. And she paid the price." The words rip from my throat like razors tearing messily through fabric. "But then again, so did I." I swing my hook up, so it is directly in front of her face.

Feelings I don't dare name churn inside of me as I bare my blackest sins to the pixie who is determined to judge me. She should. I deserve her damnation.

We both need to remember what I am and what she is. Two entire worlds apart. She's an angel, and I'm the devil.

Tink doesn't look at my metal appendage. Instead, her gaze burns into mine with open resentment and loathing. My guts twist at her expression. I put it there, but a part of me wants to kiss it away, smooth her features. To push my tongue past her lips until she submits and glazes over with desire, forgetting, or at least abandoning her hatred for lust and desire.

I return to the chair and take my position. "Let's get this over with."

Even as the minutes stretch out, I don't turn around.

I may have fucked my chances of getting Tink to break my last curse, but I'm not sure I care.

I deserve to live under a black mark. It serves me right if Tink throws me out on my ass and refuses to help me. I'll live in a starless, stormy sky, adrift without a harbor. Then again, have I ever known calm waters?

Disgust rises in me over my maudlin thoughts, but it's cut short by the buzz and burn of her tattoo gun.

Guess we are still doing this thing.

This time, I embrace the pain. I welcome it. It scorches worse than the lava searing into my flesh. It is what I've earned, and it drowns out the memories and recriminations. Mostly, it gives me something to focus on other than the image of Tink's abhorrence for me.

"Almost done." Tink's words penetrate the haze of pain and self-hatred I've been stewing in.

I grip the chair harder, the leather creaking under the pressure as she finishes the last line.

Alright old boy, keep your godsdamn hands to yourself no matter what. You can do this.

The curse shatters with a force that shakes the very bones in my body. Magic explodes through the room, slamming into me like a tidal wave, and for a moment, I can't breathe. The air crackles with energy, thickening, pushing in on me from all sides. The pain is blinding, searing through my chest, but it's more than that. It's like a weight pressing down on my very soul, crushing everything beneath it.

My eyes snap open, and Tink stares at me, wide-eyed, her hands trembling as she pulls back. The magic isn't just in the air—it's in us, in our blood, our bones, insistent, unyielding. The need is a raw, aching hunger that gnaws at my insides, demanding to be fed.

Before I can think, before I can stop myself, I'm on my feet, my body moving on instinct. I reach for her.

At the last moment, I curl my hand into a fist, forcing myself to stay rooted to the spot.

I gave her my word. I won't touch her. No matter how my blood screams for her. No matter how hard my dick is, needing to plunge into her hot, tight body.

No matter how I want to change her opinion of me, to give her something I've never given anyone else. Trust.

Tink is panting, her brows drawn in distress even as she watches me. Is she skeptical? Afraid? Or insanely turned on, wet and ready for me to take her. Her pupils are fathomless pools of ink I want to dive into, but I fucking won't.

"You know how you promised on your ship's hull you wouldn't touch me?" Tink asks, her voice hoarse.

I can barely bring myself to nod, still clamping down on all my raging desires and instincts to make her mine.

"Well, I didn't promise dick." With that, she grabs the back of my head and hauls me down and kisses me like she's drowning.

CHAPTER 14
HANDICAPABLE
TINK

The moment our lips touch, it's like gasoline meeting flame. The magic roars to life, searing through us both, and the world explodes in a blinding flash of heat and light. My breath catches in my throat, my heart slams with each beat as the energy floods my veins and presses on my skin, threatening to turn me inside out with need.

His hands are on me, rough and demanding, and I love it.

I hate him. I hate him so much. The hate pulses in me like a living beast but instead of repelling my desire, it fuels it, feeds it until it's out of control.

Gasping for air, I try to gain some distance between us, but our kisses are wild and insatiable. The sound of my gasp is drowned out by the deafening roar of magic that seems to vibrate around us.

Hook's fingers dig into my ass with a primal grip, demanding my submission. My body caves to his dominating presence, my knees buckling as he presses closer. His strong, towering figure holds me up, forcing me to concede.

I'm swept away by his essence of sea salt, spice, and masculinity. How can anyone that bad smell this fae fucking good?

The room spins, the walls closing in, and all I can see is him—dark blue eyes burning with the same desperate need that claws at my insides. All I taste is him, salt and sex and pure sin. The air is thick with the scent of him, a heady combination of cologne and sweat and raw masculinity. It tantalizes my senses and makes my heart race with excitement. Kissing him, losing myself to him feels like dying.

"Fae lords," I whisper, the words almost lost in the cacophony of magic and tension. I should push him away, stop this, but all I can think about is the way his skin feels, the way his breath mingles with mine, hot and ragged.

The curse has us in its grip, twisting our desires, amplifying every touch until it's unbearable. My wings twitch, fluttering in the wake of the magic, scattering pixie dust into the air that catches in the swirling energy, making it glow with an otherworldly light.

He presses me to the wall, and the shock of cold plaster against my wings and back is a sharp contrast to the searing heat between us. I gasp, but it's swallowed by his mouth, by the force of the kiss that's more a battle than anything else. Teeth clash, tongues fight for dominance, and all the while, the magic pushes us further, harder, until I think I might shatter from the force of it.

My fingers claw into his hair, pulling him closer, deeper, needing more, needing everything. The magic wraps my bones, insistent, unrelenting, until it's all I can do to hold on.

"I hate you," I say in between kisses before giving his lips a hard nip. I taste copper even as he continues attacking my mouth like a ravenous animal. As if he doesn't care if I hurt him. As if he'll always come back for more.

"You should." His words are nearly lost as he attacks my neck with fervor. Sparks of desire ignite and travel down cords directly connected to my center, making me wetter, more desperate by the second. "I'm a bad, bad man, and I take what I want. It's what pirates do, and you should *never* forget it."

We claw at each other's clothes until we are naked. My hunger for him triples. That devilish mouth attacks my taut nipples with a fervor that has me wriggling and moaning. Fingers slide into my wet slit and the sounds I make are wild, unhinged, and pitchy.

They pump into me and drive me up so high, so fast my head nearly flies off my body in a dizzy spiral.

I want this. I want him. Some part of me knows it's not entirely the magic.

That unvoiced fear pushes my fervor over the edge and my body breaks and shudders. I wail, coming on his skilled fingers that help me ride out my orgasm.

A sharp bite of sensation on my thigh turns my cry into one of pain.

Even in the haze of our desire, Hook jerks back. Blood drips from my bare thigh. His hook scored my skin.

Something raw flashes through his stormy gaze. It takes me a moment to recognize it—fear.

Captain James T. Hook is afraid. Afraid of hurting me.

If I weren't already shocked, he drops to his knees and kisses around my wound with delicate pressure though the pads of his fingers dig into the undamaged parts of my leg. "Forgive me," he murmurs. He grabs a gauze pad that's in reach on my worktable and presses it to the shallow cut.

He continues that way even though we are gripped by

an out-of-control sex drive. He begs for forgiveness on his knees while I let him, stunned to have him at my feet.

He tears the hook from its brace with a sharp click, tossing it carelessly to the side. The naked vulnerability of his arm's end sends a forbidden thrill through me. I don't know why I'm surprised when I see his arm bare. It's tapered, made of flesh and bone, yet I feel as if this is seeing him truly naked. His eyes turn up to meet mine in furious anguish.

I swallow down the lump in my throat, not sure what to think. Hot tingles wash over me as something inside me shifts. I can't examine what is happening too closely. The magic won't let me even if I want to.

No. No, no, he needs to stop. Stop whatever this is.

A sharp jolt of something twists inside my chest. It's more than affection. It's more than affinity.

Whatever this version of him I'm meeting is far more dangerous than any other.

This ruthless pirate captain, capable of such violence and cruelty is exposing his softer side to me, his humanity—I don't want it.

"Stop that," I order.

Hook's brows bunch up in confusion.

"You are a vicious pirate. You kill for treasure. You take what you want."

By his own admission he tricked and stole from another fae, betrayed her the way I was.

I need to remind myself as much as I need to remind him. He's the bad guy. The very fuckable bad guy. And that's all he is.

For a moment, I see something flicker in his eyes—hurt, maybe. A sliver of regret snakes through me, but then his expression hardens. His nostrils flare, and he morphs back into the version of himself I need him to be.

With a quick, brutal move, he spins me around and slams me down on the chair he just vacated. Gripping my hair, he forces my head back in a tilt, exposing my neck. My body arches in reflexive surrender, my inner muscles clenching hard. He spreads my thighs with his arm.

"Is this what you want, pixie?" he growls, giving the hair at the base of my skull a sharp but satisfying tug. "Someone you can hate and fuck? So you can walk away feeling cleaner, having rid yourself of me when I've gone?"

Yes.

But I can't say it out loud.

Something pulses deep under all my need, a kind of hurt at hearing his words.

The feeling disappears as soon as he presses the blunt end of his arm to my heated, slick center.

"What are you—" I start to ask, but he pushes his arm further in.

I cry out at the pressure. It slips into me too easily, yet as thick as the appendage jutting out between his legs. That surprises me more than I can say.

"I'm a depraved, bad man. Does this feel wrong to you, little pixie? Maybe you've even been fisted before, but you've never been wristed." There is an evil smirk even in his words.

But as he begins to move, thrusting shallowly in a crude mimicry of the act, pleasure mixes with all manner of discomforts. Still, the need rises to a feverish crescendo.

He wrenches my head around so I can see his face, even as he violates me with his appendage. But oh, how it makes me even wetter. The feeling of his arm pushing past my piercings, stretching me in ways I never thought possible, is almost too much to bear. "Is this the villain you wanted to see, sweetheart? The thief, the scoundrel who takes what he wants, and damn the consequences?" His eyes burn into mine, the electric sapphire irises almost lost to blown black pupils.

Tears sting my eyes, though whether from his words or the overwhelming sensation, I couldn't say. Everything is too much—his arm coarsely rubbing my most sensitive flesh, the hard drag of his lips on my neck, the dark taunts dripping from his wicked tongue. I'm drowning in him, this man I should despise above all others.

"Go ahead," I dare him. "Show me just how bad you can be."

His answering laugh is harsh and humorless even as he increases his pace. "Oh, I will. Starting with this sweet quim. I'll plunder it so thoroughly even your dust will taste of me."

The crude words send a shock through my core, my nails digging into his shoulders as he works me faster, harder. I'm close, so close to shattering, every muscle pulled tight as a bowstring. I just need a little more...

His arm pistons into me with a shocking speed. My mind is lost, unable to comprehend much more than the dirty delicious fire he stokes in me until I'm screaming and crying out, begging for release.

"Come for me, my little slut," he commands, his voice pure sin and seduction despite the venom in his tone. "Quake and gush on my arm like the desperate, depraved thing you are."

And I do. I come with a soundless scream, my head thrown back and wings quivering as ecstasy crashes over me in relentless waves. The force of it seems to shake the very room, magic sparking and sizzling in the air as my pleasure peaks and ebbs.

Through it all, Hook holds me up, his heavy frame an unyielding support even as he grinds his rigid length along my hip. "That's it, love," he praises darkly. "You ride it out like such a good girl for me."

I come even harder.

"Fuck, Tink. I'm about to take everything I want out of that sweet little quim of yours, and you'll have to submit. I won't bloody hold back."

His words are ominous, full of wicked promise.

Even as I come down, the curse still pulses insistently beneath my skin, demanding more, more, always more. I've barely caught my breath and already the fever is building again, the need clawing at my insides with merciless talons.

We're far from done, Hook and I. The magic will have its due.

But at this moment, as aftershocks continue to roll through me and his eyes glitter with unholy hunger, one thing becomes crystal clear.

He's a bad man. The worst.

And I want him to ruin me.

FUCKIN' AROUND

HOOK

I'm deep in Tink's hot, greedy cunt, her legs up around my sides. Even as I plunged into her with my rigid prick, her velvet hot walls fluttered and gripped at me with the echoes of her last orgasm.

The unholy squeak that I pushed up and out of her throat as I entered her is one I want to spend the rest of my days replaying in my head.

I push her knees up, spreading her wide so I can get oh so deep. My wrist is still coated in her arousal, and I slide it over her leg, painting her in her own sex and sin. Tink's beautiful sassy face goes from its usual sparkling tan to liquid honey as perspiration coats her skin.

"Fuck," I sputter as my balls tighten up. I fight for control.

I've fucked countless others, but this is different. I've never *needed* like this before. I can confidently say I'm a generous lover, and I know how to put off my own pleasure until my partner is more than ready. But Tinkerbell has me muscling every ounce of my control not to come like a prepubescent boy with his first dirty magazine.

I don't just want her wet and willing, I want to fucking destroy her. I want to burrow inside her mind, her body, leaving hooks and tattoos on her. I want to ruin her for any other, decimate, scorch the ground so I'm the only path left for her. I want her to need and crave me as much as I do her. Even as I fuck her blind, it's not enough. I need to get deeper until I'm a permanent mark on her.

I want to be Tink's curse.

"Hook," she moans, turning her head to the side, undulating under me.

I grab her chin and jerk it back, forcing her to look at me. The black winged eyeliner and smoky makeup are melting off, making her look more provocative than any adult film star. I run my thumb over her pink lips, smearing it even more.

"James." My voice is hoarse even to my ears. "Call me James."

Those emerald depths widen a little in surprise. The defiance, the hatred—it's still written on her face, but it's tempered with a vulnerability that has me hungry for more than sex.

Then her expression settles back into that lust-filled pout. She bucks her hips up, forcing me deeper as she scrapes her nails along my scalp. "James," she breathes.

My chest squeezes so tight, I wonder for half a second if I'm verging on having a heart attack. I usually don't care what anyone calls me, but *this* matters. It matters who she sees. I want her to see *me*.

And that's something I haven't felt or wanted since I was a kid on the streets of London, starving and begging for help in the slums. I learned all too fast that if I wanted something, the only way I'd get it was by taking it.

It's how I've survived.

But I want more than survival. I don't want to take. I want Tinkerbell to give me what I want. I want her to say she only wants me. She only needs me.

The thought infuriates me. In so few encounters, this little blonde has snaked power from me and now holds it in her tiny, dexterous hands.

I roar as I fuck her fast and furious, her desire turning our joining into a slippery wet ride that leaks onto the chair and our thighs.

Tink's back bows as she screams, coming on me like my good girl. Her inner muscles clench around me, the piercings adding an extra layer of delicious friction.

"James," she gasps, and the sound of my name on her lips sends a jolt of pure, primal satisfaction through me, and I'm coming harder than I ever have before. Gasping, I claw at her supple, soft body as I give her everything I have. My eyes shut and stars implode behind my lids as every muscle is wrenched and wrung out.

My pace slows but never stops. Tink's fingers brush through my hair as she kisses up my throat, across the reddened scar.

Terror grips me that this is more than just desire, more than just the raw, animalistic need that's been fueling us. It's something deeper, something I don't dare name.

But fuck, it feels like home.

Tink's nails rake down my back, scoring lines of fire that fuel the heat already coursing through me urging me to pick up the pace again. The magic hums around us, insistent, demanding, and I can't stop, won't stop until I've taken every last bit of her, until she's mine in every possible way.

CHAPTER 16

AT THE WATERING HOLE

HOOK

By the time the magic finally releases its grip on us, we're both spent, our bodies a tangled mess of limbs and sweat, our chests heaving as we try to catch our breath. The room is silent except for the sound of our breathing, and for a long moment, neither of us moves.

As we lie there, spent and satiated, I can't help but notice the way Tink's wings droop slightly, a sign of exhaustion.

I pull back slowly, slipping out of her warm body, and collapse onto the floor beside her. My heart still races, my mind still reeling from the intensity of what just happened. But there's a strange sort of clarity in the aftermath, a sense of something shifting, settling between us.

Tink rolls onto her back, her wings spread out beneath her like a fallen angel. She stares up at the ceiling, her expression unreadable, and I wonder what she's thinking. If she feels even a fraction of the confusion and turmoil that I do.

Don't be an idiot. She doesn't want you. Not past a good fucking anyhow.

Angling my head to the big front windows of her shop, the familiar steady pelt of rain hits the glass. The clouds have turned light gray with the morning dawn. Still, the world is obscured in sheets of rain and clouds so no one is likely to spy us splayed naked on Tink's tile floor.

The urge to wrap her in my arms, to hold her and brush her hair from her face is strong.

I glance at Tink, her chest rising and falling as she tries to catch her breath. She looks...peaceful.

Shifting my position to sit up, I lean back on my elbows. The curse may have released its grip on us, but I'm not ready to leave. Not yet.

I brush my fingers along her ear, marveling at the delicate studs and dangling jewels that adorn the soft skin, a beautiful reminder of her fierce, unapologetic spirit.

Tink stirs beside me, her eyes fluttering open. There's a flicker of something in her gaze—confusion, maybe regret—before she schools her expression into something more guarded. "I need to clean up," she murmurs, more to herself than to me.

"Yeah," I respond, my voice rougher than I intended. The words hang between us, heavy with unspoken tension.

She hesitates as if debating something internally. Then, as if making a decision, she pushes herself up and reaches for the blanket we stripped from the loveseat earlier.

"Water?" she offers.

That throws me. "Yes, please." I stumble over my words.

My body is nearly as drained as a mummy's after all the sweat and fluids I've released. She must be the same. I follow her to the back room where she grabs two large glasses and we fill them from the sink and drain them over and over, gasping between gulps.

My entire body sighs in relief from the hydration, but

even then the exhaustion and soreness from all the activity catches up to me. My hip rests against the counter as I sag.

Tink's eyes nervously flit to the staircase and back to me. She lives in the apartment above the shop. I bet this is the closest she's ever let anyone get to her sanctuary since that fucker Peter Pan screwed her over. I couldn't even begin to imagine what her place is like other than it would be so very..... .her.

I'm careful to keep my attention away from those steps. Her shoulders eventually drop as she relaxes.

The moment is unexpectedly ordinary. The two of us simply standing and rehydrating. She's wrapped in a blanket, while I'm still undressed, my absence of clothing emphasized by the missing hook. I'm even more naked without the covering for my wrist. Using my bare arm to pleasure her was a first for me, but the small blonde inspires a bevy of sexual inspiration.

There's a softness that's fallen over us and the fervor in which we acted out our feelings seems dissolved and transmuted.

"What?" Tink asks, her eyes rounder than usual. "You're staring at me."

My lips twitch. "You're staring at *me*."

Tink's gaze drops at that. "Yeah well, you're standing in front of me."

"Don't ever cut your hair."

Her lashes flutter in surprise.

Before she can speak, I set down my water glass and run my fingers down the waterfall waves of her platinum hair. "I've seen great beauties all around the world, but I'm finding it hard to remember someone more..." I search for the word, knowing whatever one I land on will still be insufficient. Fierce? Luminous? Magical? "Singular."

Pink stains her cheeks as she looks away. Tink can blush. I don't know why that surprises me.

Wait, yes I do. After all we just did, I think she'd have lost the ability.

"I do love the length, but it uh, gets caught in my wings." She gestures behind her.

I frown before gently nudging her soft shoulder, forcing her to turn. She glances at me over her shoulder repeatedly, as if nervous to put her back to me.

My fingers find the knots and swoops of impossibly long hair that have indeed bound around her wings. I instantly set to work unwinding and gently tugging the knots free that are looped around the iridescent chitin. In moments, I have it mostly untangled.

"You are really good at that," she breathes, likely feeling the freedom against her scalp again.

My lips tug up to one side. "Yeah well, rope and knots are a key part of running a tight ship and with one hand I have to be deft and quick should anything get out of sorts. A necessary skill."

A soft giggle escapes her.

"What?"

Tink fully turns around, adjusting the afghan around her body. "Are we actually having a conversation?"

I give her a wry smile. "Looks like."

Again, her cheeks go pink and something in my chest pinches tight. She can go from being a badass tattoo artist to a wanton sex goddess, to an endearing blushing sprite that causes a rush of protectiveness to come over me.

A ripple of unease follows.

You're in dangerous waters, Hook.

She sighs, raking a hand through her hair. "I don't know

about you, but I'm gonna need a bucket-sized tea to survive this day."

I straighten, taking that as my cue to go.

"Want me to grab you a coffee too? There's a cafe just across the street," she offers, the words tentative, testing the waters.

It's a small gesture, but the idea of her doing something so...domestic, so normal, hits me harder than I expect.

"Alright," I say, ignoring the sudden tightness in my chest.

She nods, avoiding my gaze as she disappears into the bathroom with her clothes.

I pull on my pants, my mind reeling. Am I really going to stay? There's nothing holding me here. But something about the way she looked at me—the guarded softness in her eyes—keeps me rooted to the spot. I reattach my prosthetic, adjusting the hook to my preferred angle. Besides, I'm not quite ready to walk out into that storm. Not yet.

The storm.

That means Tink has given me back the stars again. A relief so grand expands in my chest it is damned near painful.

I hear the sound of water running from the small bathroom. Curiosity gets the better of me, and I quietly follow, pausing just outside the slightly open door.

Inside, Tink leans over the sink, splashing water on her face. Her white band tee is rumpled from spending the night on the floor, but her jeans curve to her rear. The harsh fluorescent light highlights the fresh, clean lines of her features as she scrubs away the remnants of smeared makeup. The sight of her bare, makeup-free face is intimate, real.

What would it be like to see this version of Tink every

night and morning? To have her be the first thing I see when I wake up and the last before I close my eyes at night? The thought is unsettling, yet I can't shake it.

Tink catches sight of me in the mirror and startles slightly before quickly masking it. "Just washing up."

"Take your time," I say, propped against the doorframe, doing my best to sound nonchalant. "We're in no rush."

She gives me a small, almost shy nod before turning back to the mirror. I watch as she dries her face with a towel, her movements quick and efficient. The softness of her bare skin, the vulnerability of her without the armor of makeup—it affects me more than I can say.

"Be back in five minutes," she says, with a hint of a smile.

"Take your time," I repeat.

The distance between us shrinks to inches as she slips by me and a gravitational pull beckons me even closer. It feels natural to kiss her, slowly, sweetly, tracing the curve of her jaw.

But I don't. If I did that, I couldn't blame the move on a magic-fueled moment of madness. It would be real.

Tink pauses and wavers, making me think she feels the same pull too. Then she slips by.

Watching her retreating form, I know I should leave. I should gather my things and walk out that door, back into the rain-soaked streets. But something keeps me here, rooted in place, waiting.

As the tinkling door chime signals her departure, I know I'm staying for more than just coffee.

CHAPTER 17

MAKE A WISH, MAKE A WAVE

TINK

Waiting in line at the Magic Bean Cafe, I push in the piercing over my lip out of habit. A slight tremor runs through my muscles. I got rode hard and put up wet.

I close my eyes against the visual I just conjured.

Why do you do this to yourself, Tink?

I can't answer that. Just like I can't answer the question of why I broke the "no touching" rule when Hook was going to stick to his word.

The easy answer is the magic was too strong.

The truth is far more terrible than I can swallow.

I have an affinity for a literal villain. I thought this was the kind of problem reserved for girls with daddy issues.

A little tug on the back of my shirt knocks me from my thoughts.

"Oh my gosh, Libby!" I bend over to scoop the little girl in my arms instantly. I take time to hug her mother, Diana, next. I haven't seen them since Libby came in for a tattoo to give her the courage to face treatment for her illness. I've often wondered how they were doing, wishing I had some way of checking in, but I didn't want to overstep.

My hands gently wrap around Libby's shoulders. "Oh my gosh, look at you!" Shock and happiness overtake me in the absolute best way. I push back the locks of Libby's now strong and full hair. Her figure is healthy, no longer gaunt from sickness and treatment. Even her smile blasts the power of a thousand suns as if she is super aware of her glow up.

"You look amazing," I say, brushing a hand over her arm.

"Well, we have your friend to thank, of course," Diana says, smiling.

I straighten, releasing Libby's shoulders. "What?"

Diana falters, eyes darting between me and Libby. "Of course, you did so much for us too."

Libby sticks out her arm, showing off the tree of life I tattooed on her little arm. "I'm the only kid in my entire school who has a tattoo. I'm the coolest." She positively beams.

"Next," the barista calls, forcing me to break away. I order an extra large lavender hibiscus iced tea with a quarter cup of melted honey. I also order a large strong black coffee for Hook, and skip on accessorizing it with cream or sugar. I doubt that man has a sweet tooth.

I could leave, head back to the shop, but what Diana said sticks to my brain, so I wait.

Diana and Libby order before coming over.

"I got a hot chocolate," Libby announces with delight. "With whipped cream. Because I got an A on my geography test. I didn't even forget any of the fairy realms. Midnight Realm, Realm of the Roses..." She continues to recite them all.

"If you get hyper and then crash, it's your teacher's problem today," Diana says sternly, but with a hint of mischief.

"Diana," I interrupt. "What did you mean, it's thanks to my friend?"

The woman looks between me and Libby with that placid smile before it falters. "You know, your friend. Hook."

"My friend...Hook," I repeat, incredulous that the words are even emerging from my mouth.

Diana's eyes crinkle with confusion. "Yes, after we were in last time, he showed up the next day at the hospital. Said you gave him our room number." Diana's words fade away as she realizes from my expression that I have no idea what she's talking about.

"Libby, go sip your hot chocolate over at that table," Diana instructs.

The girl doesn't hesitate to seat herself and carefully pulls off the top of her treat so she can lick directly at the generous dollop of whipped cream.

Diana threads her arm through mine, her voice lowering so only I can hear. "At first, I was terrified. I mean, who wouldn't be? He looks like an absolute scoundrel. I thought he followed us to rob us, I'm ashamed to say." She ducks her head. "I told him we didn't have anything. That's when he said *you* sent him."

I shake my head even as she goes on.

"He was..." Diana pauses as if to collect the right words. "...an angel with Libby. He made her laugh off the bat with some silly jokes about fish, but I still wasn't convinced he was trustworthy. He asked permission to close the door; he had something special for Libby. I swear I was ready to raise an absolute ruckus, but I'm glad I didn't. He shut the door and pulled out one of his necklaces, it had this beautiful charm of ocean waves on it."

I knew what she referenced. The Waves of Poseidon. The turquoise waves were in a perpetual frozen state of cresting. The charm he betrayed that mermaid for. I didn't say any of that though. I let Diana go on.

"He said it protects him from serious harm and illness. That's when he took it off."

"He took it off?" I realize I sound like a parrot repeating most of what Diana says, but I'm struggling to process. None of this sounds like the Hook I know.

Diana nods. "He said you explained Libby's condition and that she could use all the help she could get, so he was there to throw in too. Then he put the necklace around Libby's neck. He told her to never take it off and to take care of it for him. He'd return for it in a month. And then he left."

"He left?"

Tink, you really need to get a hold of the English language again.

Diana nods in earnest, giving my arm a little squeeze. "Tink, the way Libby recovered over that month." Her words thicken with emotion and her eyes turn glassy. "It was nothing less than a miracle. The doctors couldn't explain it. She made a full recovery. We went from having weeks, maybe months, to Libby running around in the backyard, playing with her friends." The back of her wrist wipes away a tear.

"And then he came back?" I prompt, needing to hear the rest—dying for more information to fill the pit that's opened up in my stomach. I don't know exactly what I need from Diana, but I desperately need it.

To hear Hook's not a bad guy? Or to hear confirmation

of how he fucks this up? I'm not sure if I need my illusions shattered or sealed about the pirate captain.

Diana's lips curve in a small smile. "Two months later. We were back home at that point. I was afraid he wouldn't find us, so I gave the hospital explicit instructions to give him our home address and info if he came around looking for Libby. When he did show up, he looked...rough." Her voice drops as she shoots a glance at Libby, who is still amusing herself with the whipped cream on her fingers now.

"Rough? Rough how?" Though my brain travels to the fresh scars on his neck.

"He had bandages on his neck that were bleeding through and dark circles under his eyes. It looked like someone tried to cut his throat." Diana visibly shudders. Then she licks her lips. "I think...I think he gave up his protection for Libby." Again her words turn tight with emotion.

I don't *think* it. I know it. He forwent the Waves of Poseidon to help a sick little girl. Why does the notion make me sick to my stomach?

Diana sets her coffee cup down to face me, gripping both my arms now even as I hold the two drinks. "I misjudged your friend, Tink, and I'm so sorry. He is a good man and without him, I don't know if Libby would be here today." Tears streaming down her face, Diana holds me so tight I can scarcely draw a breath.

Or maybe I can't breathe because the oxygen around me is full of impossible ideas I can't absorb into my body.

Libby waves at me through the window as I walk away, my numb legs carrying me back to my shop.

As soon as I open the door, I know he's gone. There is an undeniable emptiness to the place without him in it. And though this parlor has been the home to my purpose, it feels like something is distinctly missing.

Setting Hook's coffee on my checkout counter, I let out a sigh, trying to rid myself of the confusion.

James T. Hook is a despicable pirate. He kills and steals, exploits my kind and openly admits it.

So what in the witchtits is he doing going around saving little girls from terminal illnesses? He gave up his protection for Libby and even paid the price with his own throat to help her.

I suck down my honey-infused floral tea, trying to drown out the chaos rolling around in my brain.

I hate him.

But I still helped him. Even when I knew the curse breaking would set off an irresistible sex bomb.

He saved a little girl. He clearly hated what Pan did to me.

I dig my palm into my eye in an attempt to relieve the pressure building in my brain.

No matter how I try to fit his pieces together, I can't make sense of Captain James T. Hook.

And what's worse, I feel the grips of an obsession and know I won't be satisfied until I do.

CHAPTER 18

SPILLING ON THE BAR

TINK

"**S**o then we fucked uncontrollably, all over the shop, and did things I'd never even read about."

I've had one too many elderflower spritzes at the Poison Apple and everything is pouring out now.

I could blame the drinks. They are beyond divine and a weakness I don't often give in to.

It's been five excruciatingly long months since Hook walked out of my tattoo parlor again. With each day that passes, my impatience, my need to see him, to demand explanations from him grow.

The fact I feel empty, hollow, and oh so very horny is an inconvenient addition to my growing tension.

I could blame the company for why I'm suddenly spilling all the gory details, since this bougie watering hole is where all my friends and clients either work or wind down.

I could blame the environment. The Poison Apple creates a comfort, a familiarity, that allows one to access their most forbidden natures.

Red velvet couches, glowing liquor bottles rising behind

the bar, and the massive live tree that extends its branches out over the lounge chairs, growing up toward the window-plated ceiling.

Belle leans in from her seat next to me. "Okay, well as the owner of the only romance bookstore in this city, I demand you give me a detailed description of it. For science." She adjusts her glasses before putting her red lips to her glass of prosecco. Also in her late twenties, we bonded the first time we met through Rap, the owner of Poison Apple. It's heartening to be part of a group of women who are entrepreneurs and business owners.

"Is that a thing with all curses?" Snow's white brow wrinkles. The bartender with onyx skin and white hair sets her ice-blue stare on me as she polishes a martini glass. She's bird-boned and almost as petite as me. "When you break them, crazy sex power grips you and forces you to be its bitch?"

"Mermaid magic is wild and untamed," Ariel's voice cuts in as she pulls a bottle of elderflower liqueur from the shelf, her red hair catching the light. She rolls her wheelchair with practiced ease, setting up a small display with another spritz Snow already made. "Mermaids are creatures of the sea, and their magic reflects that—deep, unpredictable, and dangerous. When a mermaid casts a curse, it's not just about punishment or control. It's about desire, about drawing out the most hidden parts of yourself and amplifying them to the point of madness."

Belle's eyes widen. "So it wasn't just regular crazy sex power...it was mermaid magic on overdrive?"

Ariel nods, still focusing on the display she's creating. "Exactly. When you broke Hook's curse, Tink, you unleashed all that bottled-up mermaid magic. It didn't just fade away, it surged into the nearest source—you and

Hook. It's primal, raw. It takes what's already there and cranks it up to eleven."

"Or eleven thousand," I mutter.

Belle's forehead creases. "How do you know so much about mermaid magic, Ariel?"

Ariel doesn't miss a beat, flashing a quick smile. "I have a thing for mythology and folklore. Mermaids, sirens, sea creatures—they've always fascinated me. I guess I've just picked up a lot over the years from reading and research."

Belle nods, seemingly satisfied with the explanation. I shift in my seat, processing everything. "So...what happened between us wasn't just us. It was the curse."

Ariel's gaze on me is steady. "Partly, yes. But mermaid magic doesn't create something from nothing. It only amplifies what's already there. The curse might have triggered it, but the connection, the attraction—that was real. That was all you."

"So," Snow starts hesitantly, "if you knew breaking the first curse set off this uncontrollable lust bomb, why did you agree to do it for the second time?"

"Because!" I cry out, throwing my hands in the air. "I'm a terrible fucking person."

Snow and Belle exchange a look.

Okay, I *definitely* should have stopped two spritzes ago.

"Or," Belle adds diplomatically, patting my arm, "you like him?"

A series of snorts and grunts of outrage explode from my nostrils.

"He saved a little girl," Belle points out.

I gulp more of the floral liqueur and try not to think about that confusing piece of the puzzle.

"The next time he comes in, I'll say no." My words slur a little.

"Tink," Snow tries to interrupt, but I forge on.

"I'll say 'get out of here, *you*. Hit the bricks, buddy. I ain't helping.'"

"Tink," Belle says with a little more insistence, her voice tight.

"I'll be like 'get your sexy self away from me. I don't want none of it.'"

"Anyone I know?" a familiar raspy voice asks.

My gut clenches. Heat engulfs me before a sweep of ice chills my body. I slowly turn in my seat. Hook stands there, his presence dominating the space even in this crowded bar. His dark eyes glint with amusement, but there's something unreadable there too.

"Hook," I manage to say, my voice barely above a whisper. My body betrays me, a flush creeping up my neck as the memory of our last encounter floods my mind. I can still feel the imprint of his hands on my skin, the way he took me apart and put me back together again.

"Sounds like I arrived just in time," he says, his voice low and rough, sending a shiver down my spine. "I can help you cast off whatever poor bastard has had the idiocy to cross you."

"Yeah, idiocy," I echo.

Hook steps closer, his gaze sweeping over me, taking in the flushed state of my cheeks, and probably the slight slur in my words. "You've had quite the evening, haven't you, Tink?" he murmurs. I can't tell if it's a taunt or if that is a fondness twinkling in his eye.

I open my mouth to retort, to tell him to get lost, but the words catch in my throat. Instead, I just stare up at him, feeling all the anger, the confusion, and the desire I've been bottling up for the past five months bubble to the surface.

Of all the times for him to show up.

I've spent many nights drinking reasonably at the Poison Apple since I last saw him. Does he come upon me then? Noooo. He has to show up when I'm three spritzes in and spilling all the bloody details of our trysts.

Bloody? Oh my fae lords, I even sound like him now.

I need another drink.

Or maybe an exorcism.

A manic energy grips me. Probably because I just over-shared all the dirty details of our arrangement and Snow, Belle, and Ariel are currently staring at us.

"Okay then, so time to work." I smile too brightly at the gals. "No rest for the wicked." I go to stand but end up on wobbly knees. Hook catches me and pulls me to his strong side. His hot, muscled body pressing into mine only turns my knees weaker.

"Perhaps we put off the joy of you stabbing me a million times with a needle until you're a little more...rested."

"I'm fine," I pout, waving him off and escaping that delicious masculine smell that already has my panties dampening. "I can do it. You don't think I can do it?" My tone turns belligerent. I can hear that I sound like a child, but I can't stop it. Memories of him suggesting he'd go to someone else still sting my pride. There's no one better than me. He of all people needs to know that.

He confessed I was the only one who could help him the last time I saw him, but my drunken brain has glommed onto the moment when he put me down and refuses to let go.

Pixie dust begins to shimmer around me, and I realize my wings have been flapping with open agitation.

Hook glances at Snow, who's still watching us with her icy blue stare. "I've got her tab," he says, sliding a few bills across the bar. "And I'll take her home."

"What if I don't want to go home?" I counter, doubling down on being petulant.

A dark gleam sparks in Hook's eye. As plain as day, I can see the many ideas he has about how to handle me or how to get me home. All of them involve force or coercion.

"What's going on here?" a female voice interrupts. Rap strides out from her back office. The banana blonde mohawk with rainbow streaks does nothing to mitigate her take-no-shit attitude. The heavy black eyeshadow only further broadcasts that she'd kick anyone's ass at any time if she deemed it necessary. Or maybe that's her shit-kicker combat boots.

I raise my brows at Hook. Now he's in for it.

"I was just offering to take this young lady home," Hook says in an overly polite tone, his gaze never breaking from mine.

"Hook," Rap says with recognition.

He finally turns to my friend and fellow business owner. "Rapunzel."

Hook used her full name, and she didn't even bat an eyelash. *Whoa.*

"You owe me a chance to earn my money back from that last poker game," she says, a sly half smile creeping up her face though it never reaches her eyes.

"And I believe you still owe me a bottle of 1904 Flying Dutchman rum."

Rap tilts her head. "That I do." With a nod to Snow, the petite girl pulls a bottle off the shelf and hands it over to Rap, who then gives it to Hook. "Will I get a chance to earn my money back while you're in town?"

Hook looks down at me, my skin heating under his intensity. "Not this time, Rap. I've got other business to attend to."

"Good on ya then," Rap says, patting him before heading back to the bar to talk with Snow.

"Shall we?" Hook asks, extending an arm and gesturing forward with the bottle. The cold of his hook meeting my naked back sends a wash of goosebumps along my skin.

I want to argue, to tell him I don't need his help, but the truth is I'm too drunk to make it home on my own. Hook leads me toward the exit.

At the last moment, I veer away.

"Givemeasecond." It comes out a mumbled slur. I make my way over to the massive live tree. I glance at the bar but none of the girls are paying me any attention as Rap engages them. I walk around the trunk until I'm mostly out of sight.

"Miss you," I whisper before hugging the rough bark.

Feeling only slightly self-conscious but more satisfied, I trip back toward Hook. I avoid his intense gaze all the way out the door.

The cool night air hits me like a splash of cold water, clearing my head just enough to realize the gravity of the situation. I'm alone with Captain Hook, the pirate who's been haunting my thoughts and dreams for months. The man who left without a word.

As we step out into the street, I notice the storm gathering overhead. Thick, ominous clouds roll across the sky, blotting out the stars. The air is heavy, charged with the promise of rain. A few tiny droplets hit my bare skin.

We walk in silence, the tension between us crackling like electricity. My heels click against the pavement and I stumble slightly, cursing under my breath. Hook's arm is around my waist in an instant, steadying me.

"You're a little sloshed, aren't you, love?" he mutters,

but there's no malice in his voice. If anything, he sounds amused.

"Thanks for the observation, Captain Obvious," I slur, but I don't pull away from his grip. It feels too good, too solid, too real.

"Any particular occasion?" he asks.

I shrug. "I'm a grown fairy. I do what I want." It has nothing to do with getting so strung out with this waiting game of not knowing when he would come back that I had to get out and blow off some steam before I crawled out of my skin.

"That you do," he says, almost under his breath.

Is he referring to when I jumped him the last time, even though he managed to hold back? My head starts to swim, so I stop wondering.

A sudden crack of thunder makes me jump, and I grip Hook's shirt. The storm is right above us now, the wind picking up, swirling leaves and debris at our feet. My hair whips my face, getting tangled in the breeze as we hurry down the deserted streets.

As we near my shop, fear flashes through me. The thought of letting him upstairs, into my personal sanctuary, makes my palms sweat. "I'm not letting you up," I say quickly.

"Of course, not," he says. As if it never crossed his mind. As if he knows what it means to me and would never push.

A pirate respecting boundaries.

I must be drunker than I thought.

After what feels like an eternity, we reach the back alley door to Inked by Tink. The rain is coming down harder now, soaking through my clothes. I fumble with my keys, but Hook takes them from my hand and unlocks the door with ease. He doesn't follow me inside though. Instead, he hovers at the threshold, his expression unreadable.

"Go on," he urges softly. "Wash your face, get some sleep. We'll talk in the morning."

I blink up at him, taken aback by the unexpected respect in his tone. For all his roughness, there's something almost...tender in the way he looks at me.

The wind howls down the alley, rattling the windows of my shop as lightning flashes, illuminating the sharp angles of Hook's face. The rain is coming down in sheets now, and yet there he stands, as if the weather is just an extension of him, swirling and raging, but unable to touch the core of who he is.

Before I can say another word, he's gone, swallowed up by the storm.

HE KNOWS HER FAVORITE DRINK

HOOK

I push open the door to Inked by Tink, the bell chiming softly as I step inside. The storm I carry with me covers the morning sun.

The place is quiet, almost too quiet. The tension in the air is thick enough to cut with a knife. It's been five long months since I walked out of here, and I recognize the damage that's been done in that time.

The confusion, the hurt—it's all there, bubbling under the surface. Or rather, boiling over in the bar last night.

Tink's in the back, where I knew she would be. She's standing by the counter, staring at something on her phone with a frown etched into her brow.

Her head snaps up, and those blue-green eyes of hers lock onto me with a mix of emotions I can't quite place. I used to think they sparkled like emeralds dipped in the sky, but I realize now they reflect the colors of the most beautiful oceans I've sailed.

Bloody hell on a witch's tit. Tink looks absolutely illegal. Wearing a scandalously short plaid skirt over her fishnets and boots, and a cropped white collared shirt, she is the spitting image of a naughty schoolgirl. The punk rock piercings and heavy makeup only add to her edgy appearance, accentuated by those thick-framed glasses that I've developed an unhealthy obsession with.

My cock thickens in my slacks immediately. I swallow hard, a sad attempt to calm my body. How in the seven seas am I to control myself?

"Morning," I say, holding up the drink and the bag. "Figured you might need this."

She doesn't move, just stands there, eyes narrowed as if trying to figure out what I'm up to. Finally, she crosses her arms over her chest, her posture defensive. "What's in the bag?"

"Hangover meds," I answer, stepping closer. "And your favorite drink. Lavender hibiscus tea with a quarter cup of melted honey, right?"

Her eyes widen slightly in surprise. Tink's wings twitch and flutter behind her, a clear sign of her agitation. The movement is endearing, and I find myself fighting back a smile at the way her body betrays her emotions, even as she tries to maintain a cool, unaffected facade.

"How did you know my favorite drink?" Her voice is dark with suspicion.

"I asked the barista at the Magic Bean across the street. Since you are a regular, they know your order."

Her expression volleys between softening over the surprise treat, and forbidding hardness.

"Why are you here, Hook?"

I set the drink and the bag down on the counter, taking a moment to really look at her. She's tired, that much is clear, but there's a spark in her eyes that wasn't there last night. A defiance. As if she wants to fight me. Or maybe fuck me. . .

Down, Hook.

"Because we have unfinished business," I say, my voice low and steady. She should know.

The last tattoo.

The last curse.

The last key. I found it.

"I'm all full up today," she says, something like guilt flitting through her eyes. "Packed schedule."

"I've no doubt. You're a popular lady." I push the drink into her hand. "I'll come back later. But I figured you needed this now."

Her shoulders drop as she submits to my offering with a mumbled, "Thank you."

She downs the pills and sucks down nearly half her drink.

I glance around the shop, my attention lingering on the framed tattoo designs on the walls, the organized chaos of her workspace.

Leaning against the counter, I turn my attention to Tink, thinking of last night. The desire to peel away her layers, exploit every secret, revisit every vulnerability she's tried to bury grips me until I have to ask.

"That tree in Poison Apple..."

Tink's shoulders tense, fingers curling around her iced drink as she pulls it into her body protectively.

"It's yours, isn't it? The one that wanker drained of magic."

"Yes. That was my tree," she says softly, her voice laced with resignation.

"And now it's here," I murmur, more to myself than to her.

"Rap brought it here," Tink continues, her voice steady but tinged with a sorrow that cuts deeper than I expected.

"She knew what it meant to me. It was dead, but she managed to revive it just enough. It's not my home anymore, though. But I like being near it."

She laughs wryly before all mirth slides off her face. Her fingers drum on the cup she holds.

"It has some magic to it," I point out. I know it. I've always known it. I've visited the Poison Apple several times over the years, and I can pick out magic the way a curator can spot a treasure amidst a heap of trash—a skill I've developed.

"I don't know how Rap did it," Tink shakes her head. "But it's hers now, not mine."

I consider her words, feeling the weight of them settle into my bones. A wave of anger rises on her behalf, tangled with something else, something more unsettling. The idea that something so central to who she is, her very essence, could be reduced to this. A centerpiece at a bar.

"It's nice," she hurries to say as if she can read my dark thoughts. "It's not my home, but it's as close as I'll ever get to that feeling again."

That only angers me further. Tink deserves more than to have her home destroyed by some little prick and then have the reminder set in her vicinity to taunt her with the past, the mistakes, the heartbreak.

It takes a moment to realize I'm sliding my fingers along the cold steel of my hook.

I know all too well what that feels like.

An idea grips me. It's ludicrous. Unnecessary. Absolutely unwelcome.

But it digs its hooks into my mind as deeply as a fishhook through the gills, making it hard to breathe as I'm captured by the possibilities.

I keep my expression neutral, not wanting to reveal too

much of my thoughts. But the idea lingers, growing roots in the back of my mind. A literal seed of a thought.

For a moment, there's silence between us, the weight of everything unsaid hanging in the air. I can see the turmoil in her eyes, the way she's struggling with the emotions I've stirred up.

A part of me wants to reach out, to pull her close and tell her everything I feel. What I'm thinking. What I'm planning.

Instead, I push off the counter and close the distance between us, stopping just short of touching her. The intensity in my gaze is enough—I know she can feel it. I want her. I've wanted her all these past five months.

She swallows, forcing a small, shaky smile as she steps back, putting that sliver of distance between us that she seems to need so badly. "Thank you for the tea," she says, her voice wavering slightly. "And the meds. I guess I'll see you later, Captain."

I hesitate just for a moment, feeling the pull between us, the desire to bridge that gap she's created. But I nod instead, keeping my voice low and rough. "Aye, you will."

With that, I turn and walk out into the storm, the door closing softly behind me. The rain is relentless, soaking through my clothes in seconds, but I don't pay it any attention. My mind is on her, on that tree, on the idea that's taken root deep in my gut.

Tinkerbell thinks she's putting distance between us, that she's keeping me at arm's length. But she doesn't know how much I'm questioning. How much I'm willing to entertain the thought of wanting something a pirate shouldn't want—land under my feet, a place to weigh anchor.

CHAPTER 20
NEVER BELIEVE A BAD MAN

HOOK

The neon "closed" sign of Inked by Tink casts a blue glow into the inky darkness of the street. Cold rain pelts me as I open the door and head straight to the back room of the tattoo shop.

The pixie, still dressed like a walking felony, shuts the door behind us.

I reach for the hem of my shirt, pulling it over my head, and toss it onto the chair nearby.

Tink's gaze flickers down to my chest, and she licks her lips.

Oh fae lords, if she starts that now, I'm never going to survive. Fuck the curse. I want to push that hot pleated skirt up and rail her six ways from Sunday.

"Where's the key?" Tink asks, her tone clipped, keeping things strictly business.

I pull out the last key from my pocket and place it on the tray she's laid out. "Right here. The final piece."

I made a trade with a Sphinx—a timeless entity that demands a sacrifice for every favor.

It is the way of magic. Magic for magic. An energy

exchange to keep things in balance. I parted with a phoenix feather, a relic of resurrection, to obtain this key. The price was steep, but it was necessary.

Tink's fingers hover over the key, and for a moment, I think she's going to back out. But then she grabs it, her hands steady even as her eyes flick up to meet mine.

"Sit down."

I assume the position on her chair, putting my back to her. I wish it was like the first time when I could face her. I want to watch the intent way her eyes narrow as she focuses on recreating the third key on my body.

For the past five months, I've been dreaming of those elegant, small hands pumping my cock with vigor. Of feeling her pants of desire against my ear, knowing I'm driving her closer to her release.

"You lied," Tink says, interrupting the fantasy that now has me hard as a flagpole.

"About what?" I sift through all the lies I've told her.

"That you're a bad man," she says lightly.

I start to twist, but she slaps my bare shoulder. "Don't move."

"What are you talking about?" I ask, my voice a grouse.

"I know what you did. For Libby."

I stiffen. Though that could be from the first touch of her tattoo gun. Witchtits, I forgot the potency of the pixie dust against my curses. I bite my tongue to keep from crying out.

"I don't know what you are talking about," I grunt.

"Sure you do." She says it with a casual air like she's got me all figured out. "You saved a little girl. You even gave her your charm of protection. I know that's why you have that scar on your neck."

My teeth grind in frustration. If that damn port guard

had just taken the bribe like the others, none of this would have happened. Instead, he raised the alarm, putting our ship and cargo at risk.

He fought like a cornered animal, but we managed to subdue him and silence the alarm. Then, one of my crew let the kid loose. Before I knew it, the boy had a knife, and I was clutching my neck, trying to stop the bleeding. Even then, I kicked him in the face and knocked him out.

The mission went sideways. We had to get me to a medical facility because our ship's doctor couldn't handle it. It took two magic healers to fix me up.

If I'd been wearing the Waves of Poseidon, I would have likely caught his wrist before he could slice me. Or at the very least, I could have recovered in a third of the time with the charm's healing factor.

The crew wanted to kill the kid for what he did to me, but I stopped them.

"You don't know anything about me." The words come out as harsh as I mean them. I never planned on Tink finding out what I did for Libby.

Tink only hums in disagreement.

"I didn't do it for her," I say, the lie heavy on my tongue. "I did it because her mother was so damn judgmental. She took one look at me and thought she had me all figured out. I wanted to prove her wrong, make her see she shouldn't judge a man on sight."

"So you wanted to prove to her that you're a good guy?" Tink doesn't buy it. I can hear it in the way she snorts softly.

"No," I snap, my frustration rising. "I wanted to make her uncomfortable. Watching her squirm while I turned out to be the opposite of what she expected—it was satisfying."

Tink's tattoo gun halts for a moment. "So, you're telling

me you helped a dying little girl just to make her mother uncomfortable?"

"Yes," I hiss, though even I can hear how weak and irrational it sounds. I'm grasping at straws, clinging to the idea that I'm the villain in this story. But the truth is, that little girl's smile when she put on that necklace, the way her eyes lit up like she had the world at her feet—it did something to me. Something I don't want to admit.

"And the protection charm?" Tink presses. Her voice is softer now, more probing. "You gave it to her, knowing it could cost you?"

I grit my teeth. "It was a trinket. I had others."

"You're lying," she says, and there's no accusation in her tone, just certainty. "You wanted to help her because deep down, you're not as bad as you want to believe."

"Stop it," I growl, the anger flaring up again, not at her, but at myself. "I'm a pirate, Tinkerbell. A villain. I take what I want and damn the consequences."

She's silent for a moment, then the tattoo gun hums back to life. "If you say so." Doubt laces her words.

I bite down on a retort, feeling the sharp sting of the needle as she starts on the final key. The pain is nothing compared to the anger simmering just below the surface. She doesn't know what she's talking about. She doesn't understand what it means to be a pirate, to do the things I've done. Saving that girl was a moment of weakness, a lapse in judgment. It doesn't change who I am.

"I'm a bad man, Tink," I say, my voice low and hard. "I take what I want. I kill without remorse. Don't mistake one act of mercy for something it's not."

She pauses, her hand hovering over my back, and I can feel her gaze burning into me. "You keep saying that," she murmurs, almost as if to herself. "But I'm not so sure I believe you anymore."

I grit my teeth, feeling the curse stirring within me, the storm that's been my constant companion threatening to break free. "You don't need to believe me," I snap. "Just finish the job."

For a moment, there's only the sound of the tattoo gun and the crackle of tension in the air. Then, she starts talking again, her voice softer, more measured. "You know, I've spent my whole life trying to prove I'm not just some silly little pixie. That I'm more than what people expect me to be."

I stiffen, not sure where she's going with this. "What's your point?"

"My point," she says, her voice growing firmer, "is that maybe you're more than what you've let yourself become. Maybe you don't have to be the villain in every story."

I bark out a harsh laugh, the sound bitter even to my ears. "You think you can fix me, Tink? You think a few kind words and a pretty face can change who I am?"

She keeps working, the hum of the tattoo gun filling the silence.

"No, I don't think I can fix you," she says softly. "But I don't think you're as broken as you want everyone to believe, either."

The words hit like a punch to the gut. I open my mouth to tell her she's wrong, to remind her of all the terrible things I've done, but the curse chooses that moment to rear its ugly head. The storm inside me surges, sucking the breath from my lungs.

Tink gasps, her hand slipping as the magic roars to life, the energy in the room shifting from simmering tension to full-blown chaos. It builds into the same uncontrollable hunger, the same raw, primal need that's gripped us before, only this time it's more intense, more consuming.

Not because of the magic, but because I think of her before my eyes even open in the morning. Because her face is the last thing on my mind before I fall asleep. Because my fingers itch even as they are wrapped around the helm, wishing they were skating along her skin. Because that laugh has burrowed inside my chest where it lives now. Because coming to her feels like coming home, like stepping onto my ship after too many weeks on land—a sense of belonging and completion that I've never known anywhere else.

"Hook..." she whispers, her voice tight with both fear and desire.

"I think it's time I remind you," I rasp, my hands clenching into fists as I fight against the overwhelming urge to take her, to claim her right here and now. The storm is breaking free, and there's nothing either of us can do to stop it. "I'm a bad man."

I grab her wrist and yank her down onto my lap, the tattoo gun clattering to the floor.

She opens her mouth, but I don't give her the chance to protest. My lips crash against hers, a battle for dominance as the magic pushes us closer, harder. Her hands are on my chest, nails digging into my skin. Her wings flutter wildly, scattering pixie dust that catches in the air, making the magic burn even brighter. She trembles under my touch, not from fear, but from the same desperate need that's clawing at my insides.

"I want you," I murmur. "So I'm taking you."

She gasps, her back arching as I drag my mouth down her throat, biting at the delicate skin there, marking her as mine.

"It's the curse," she whispers.

"The bloody fuck it is." My control snaps. With a growl, I throw her on the chair, hitting the pedals to recline it as I roughly push up Tink's skirt.

For fuck's sake, she's wearing garters to hold up her fishnets. Slamming my eyes shut, I grunt and grab my length through my pants. I'm a grown godsdamn man, but I almost shot my load at the sight of Tink spread out with those pink panties clinging to the outline of her delectable pussy. A dark spot at the center where she's already wet. When I open my eyes, the dark spot is even bigger.

Fae fucking hell.

I'm so hurried to free my cock that I accidentally cut my pants with my prosthetic, only adding to my ire and fervor.

Even though it still shakes, I slide my hook between Tink's pussy and the sheer cloth before slicing it away. She whimpers and shivers uncontrollably as I unwrap her perfect wet quim with precision.

Cool air hits my exposed hardness as I shove my pants down, but then I push right into the scalding pink petals of Tink's precious cunt.

Tink cries out as I slam into her to the hilt while her legs kick. I show no mercy, pistoning into her impossible tightness. Tink claws at the chair, at me, crying out the most obscene moans and curses. Giving into my primal urges, I reach into her waterfall of hair and close a hand at the base of her scalp, yanking her head. She arches into me as she yelps.

"Did you wear the fishnets for me, little girl?" I pant and grunt, continuing to punish her little quim. "To tempt a pirate like me?"

"Yes," she breathes.

I'll never tire of having her at my mercy. Of forcing her to submit to my desire for her.

"This little schoolgirl outfit, was it meant to torture me?"

She makes a strange sound I don't understand at first. Then I realize she's laughing. "It worked, didn't it?" she asks with far too much glee and satisfaction.

Oh, I'll show this brat what she's gotten herself into. The crack of my hand meeting her bare bottom causes her to jerk and cry out. I continue to land blow after blow until her bottom is a bright, angry red.

Though it pains me to do so, I withdraw from her dripping cunny. The whimper she releases is pathetic. Little pixie is always hungry for me.

So I lift her up and put her feet back on the ground. She blinks in confusion until I push her down to her knees. Her eyes turn glassy as she licks her lips.

"Open up like a good girl and take that cock."

CALL ME WHORE
TINK

"What if I don't?" I taunt, my voice a challenge, daring him to push me further, to take me beyond my limits. There's a wildness in me, a need to see just how far we can go, how much we can push each other before we both break.

Hook's grip tightens in my hair, jerking my head back. His eyes blaze with that familiar, dangerous light. "You don't want to be a good girl?" he growls, his voice low and rough, sending a shiver of anticipation down my spine. "Then you'll be my dirty little slut. My filthy, naughty schoolgirl who's been dying for a lesson."

The words hit me like a jolt of electricity, sending a rush of heat through me. There's something intoxicating about the way he talks to me, the way he strips away all the pretense and brings out the darkest parts of myself. I crave it, need it. The dirty words—the way he reduces me to nothing but raw need—make me more powerful, more in control of my pleasure than I have ever been before.

His cock presses against my lips, and I don't hesitate. I

take him into my mouth, tasting him, savoring the salt and musk.

Hook thrusts deep, pushing past the point of comfort, but I don't care. I attempt to relax my throat while hollowing my cheeks to suck him off.

"Take it, you little whore," he growls, his voice thick with lust. He thrusts deeper, making me gag. Tears sting the corners of my eyes. "You like being used like this, don't you? You want to be bad, so I'll spank that little ass until you cream your panties."

I moan around him, the vibration spurring him on. My fingers dig into his thighs, my nails scoring his skin as I try to take him even deeper, desperate to please him, to show him just how much I love being his. The good girl turned bad just for him.

"Touch yourself," he demands, the words a low growl. "I want you to come while you choke on me. Show me how much you love sucking my dick."

My hand slides between my legs, finding my slick heat, and I rub at my clit, the sensation nearly overwhelming. The combination of his rough, degrading words, the way he fills my mouth, the sharp sting of his hook against my skin —it's all too much, and I spiral toward release, my body trembling with the intensity of it.

"That's it," he grunts, his voice thick with pleasure as he watches me work myself over, his cock still moving in and out of my mouth, every thrust bringing me closer to the edge. "You're mine. All mine. You were made for this, weren't you? Made to take me down your throat, to spread your legs and beg for more."

I'm lost in it now, lost in the way he talks to me, the way he pushes me to be more, to embrace the depravity, the raw, unfiltered pleasure that courses through my veins. It's freeing, liberating, and I've never felt more powerful, more in control of my pleasure than I do in this moment.

His pace quickens as he loses control. His grip tightens in my hair, his cock throbbing against my tongue. He's close, and so am I, the tension winding tighter and tighter in my core until it's all I can do to hold on, to keep from shattering beneath the force of it.

"Fuck, Tink." His words take on an almost panicked urgency. "Swallow it all. Take it. Take it like the good little cumslut you are."

The hot rush of his release hits the back of my throat, and I swallow it down, savoring the taste, the feel of him filling me. It's messy, brutal, and I fucking love it.

My own release is close, but I need something more, something darker, something that will push me over the edge.

"Your wrist," I pant, pulling back just enough to speak, my breath hitching at the sheer depravity of what I'm about to ask for. "Use it on me. Please. I need it."

It's so wrong, but I've dreamed of it ever since that night.

Hook hesitates for a moment, still gripping my hair. I see the battle in his eyes—the tension between control and desire. It only makes me want him more.

"You're sure?" he asks, his voice thick with a dark, dangerous edge.

"Yes," I breathe, my voice trembling with fear and anticipation. "I need it."

He doesn't need more encouragement. With a rough yank, he pulls me up from the floor, spinning me around and pushing me against the counter.

My breath catches as he slides his cock into my pussy

from behind, filling me completely, fogging my brain with lust. I whimper with both satisfaction and disappointment.

This isn't what I asked for.

Even as he rocks into me, he reaches for something. The scent of coconut oil reaches my senses. I use it as a natural aftercare for a tattoo but right now I'm being slathered with the stuff as he prepares the tight ring of muscles of my rear.

This wasn't part of the plan, but I find it hard to find my voice to protest.

Oh fae lords, I don't know if I can do this.

Hook starts with a finger, pushing past the resistance. I cry out, the sensation both foreign and intensely satisfying. He works me, opens me, relaxes me until he can add a second, and eventually a third. The stretch is intense, almost too much. Still, I relish the burn, the way my body opens up to him.

Then his fingers disappear as another appendage begins to work its way in.

Oh my holy fucking fae lords, he's using his bare wrist.

My brain jerks to a halt as I forget how to breathe. The noise that escapes my throat is a combined moan and sob, and it only fuels him further.

"Gods, you're filthy," he growls, his voice rough and full of dark promise as he thrusts into me. "My dirty little slut, taking it all like the naughty girl you are."

The words send a thrill through me, and I push back against him, desperate for more, for all of him. The sensation of being filled in both places, of his thick cock pounding into me while his wrist works me from behind, pushes me beyond anything I've felt before. Every thrust drives me closer to the edge. The dual sensations send electric shocks of pleasure careening up my spine.

I'm lost in it, in him. My mind goes blank as the pleasure builds, amplified by the curse. My body is on fire, every nerve ending alight with sensation, with the delicious stretch and the relentless friction. I can't think, can barely breathe, but it doesn't matter. All that matters is the way he's taking me, the way he's owning every part of me.

"Yes," I gasp. The words spill out in a desperate plea. "Yes, yes, yes."

He growls in response, his pace becoming more urgent, more demanding. "You like that, little pixie? Being stuffed full of me?"

I can't answer. My only response is a broken gurgle as he thrusts into me harder, his wrist working me deeper. It's too much and not enough all at once, my body straining to take it, to absorb the pleasure coursing through me.

"You're mine. Do you understand that? My Tinkerbell."

My entire body seizes, a scream ripping from my throat as I shatter, the pleasure so intense it borders on agony. He follows me over the edge, his hips jerking as he spills, the heat of his release searing through me.

"Again," I whisper, even as my body is wracked with aftershocks. "Don't stop."

A dark, twisted smile curves his lips. He doesn't need to be asked twice.

CHAPTER 22

SUNNY DAYS, CHASING THE CLOUDS AWAY

HOOK

"**I**'m thirsty," Tink whispers, her voice soft, almost hesitant. As if that's not what she wanted to say at all.

We collect ourselves off the floor and begin the hunt for our clothing. I make sure to right the fringe lamp we knocked over and straighten a couple of pictures even as I grab my boots.

It's about sunrise, not that I'd be able to see it with the storm. Shock spills over me when I glance out the window.

The sky is clear. Something thick and intense lodges in my throat.

"Hook?" she asks.

I'm up and at the window. I don't give a flying fae if someone walks by and sees me stark naked. My fingers skim down the cool, smooth glass, marveling at what I'm seeing.

"The sky..." is all I can get out.

"We broke the last curse," Tink reminds me gently.

I nod and swallow hard. "I know, I just...I supposed I

never truly believed I'd see it again, unencumbered by clouds and storm. It's more beautiful than I remember." Bright orange streaks filter up into the fast-receding darkness.

Fae fucks, why is it hard to breathe all of a sudden?

Tink doesn't say anything. She just stands next to me, stark naked as well. The weight of her gaze settles on my cheek, but I can't break myself away from the dawn just yet.

When I finally drink in my fill, I turn to the pixie beside me. She gives me a half smile before she turns and makes her way to the back.

Tink's wings wave rather than flutter. As if they are stretching from exhaustion and overuse. Beneath them, her small, perfect ass is as petite as the rest of her. Even in the shadows I can see it's bright red from our activities.

Satisfaction curls in me.

Then Tink picks up her clothes off the floor, clutching them to her chest. "You should rehydrate too," she says, looking over her shoulder.

I catch the perfect profile of that pert little nose, and something in my chest tightens again. Like the Kraken itself has wrapped its suckers around me and squeezed everything out of me.

Tink opens the door to the backroom and disappears.

I stand there, blinking stupidly for a moment.

Is she saying what I think she's saying?

"You coming?" a voice filters from the backroom with a little snap of impatience to it.

I don't wait for another invitation. I go after her, only to step on my pant leg, slipping and stumbling, almost crashing to the ground.

"Pull it together, old boy," I chastise myself after I've regained my footing.

It doesn't keep me from rushing after the naked pixie goddess to the backroom and taking the staircase up, two steps at a time.

CHAPTER 23
HOLD ME UNDERWATER
TINK

*W*hat are you doing inviting the pirate up into your *home? Have you lost your little fairy mind?* My common sense screams at me, causing my throat to tighten.

Still, I slip on a silk robe covered in a floral print. My wings slip through the holes in the back, spreading and stretching. Twin satisfying aches resonate through my wings to my bones. I'm sore and exhausted but so very fucking satisfied.

The clomp of a man who has no need to hide his footfalls ascends the stairs until Hook stands in my apartment. It's almost comical seeing the rough, scary pirate at my threshold, barefoot, with his clothes and boots held in front of his junk. He studies me, his eyes narrowed and mouth slightly parted as if he's never seen anything like my place.

I'm more than a little proud of it. Plants burst from every corner and crevice, and flowerpots hang from the ceiling and curl against the windows in attempts to drink up any daylight. It even smells like a botanic hothouse—fresh dark soil and fragrant flowers.

I've already pulled out a couple of glasses and filled them with water. "Something wrong?" I croak.

I meant it when I said I was thirsty. He drained me of all moisture from the inside out.

"It's beautiful," he says with open awe. "You've made a perfect oasis."

Despite my exhaustion from our fuckfest, my wings flutter with pride and joy. I may have lost my last home, but I built a second, extraordinary one that brings me joy.

I'm also a little surprised by his appreciation. I like bright pastel colors, and the place is unforgivably feminine.

"Hmm, most guys think my place is too girly."

I'd peg him for a masculine wood planks and dark colors only kind of guy.

He snorts, even as his eyes roam across my apartment. "Sounds like a heap of little boys clinging to their bollocks to prove to themselves they are men. But I am a man who appreciates treasure, and that's exactly what this place is. A treasure."

Heat suffuses my cheeks as an invisible force strangles my heart.

Captain Hook is here, in my space, in my carefully curated world. The last time I let someone in like this...

A whisper of fear spirals through me.

He can't take this treasure from me. He has no reason to destroy my home. Not to mention it's not at all the same as my magic homestead that Peter ruined. Yet there is an echo here of that young naive girl who wanted to impress a boy with her special place.

You are a grown woman who pays rent in the big city. It's not the same at all.

I walk over and hand him a full water glass. Hook has to drop his personal effects to take it, those dark stormy blues now raking over my form. I greedily gulp the cool water, ignoring the heat he's causing to rise in my blood.

Must still be the effects of that curse breaking.

Liar. The curse magic has long passed.

I take his glass and refill both of them, and we chug some more.

"Thank you," he says, handing it back. "I guess I better..." he trails off as he reaches for his pants.

"Stay," I say, the word slipping out before I can stop it.

Hook's hand freezes mid-reach, his eyes locking onto mine. The tension between us crackles in the air, thick and heavy with everything that's happened, everything that's been said—and unsaid. For a moment, neither of us moves, the silence stretching out as I battle with my conflicting emotions.

"Why?" he asks, his voice low, almost cautious, as if he's afraid to break the fragile truce that's formed between us.

I swallow hard, trying to find the right words. I'm not even sure why I want him to stay, why the thought of him leaving right now feels so wrong. It's not just the afterglow of what we did, not just the physical connection that still lingers between us. There's something deeper, something I'm not ready to face but can't ignore either.

"You don't have to go," I murmur, barely recognizing the softness in my voice. "It's late or early, and I don't work today and...you're exhausted. We both are."

He studies me for a long moment, those stormy blue eyes of his searching mine as if he can uncover some hidden motive. But I don't have one—not really. At least, not one I'm ready to admit to myself.

He finally nods, the tension in his shoulders easing just slightly. "Alright. I'll stay."

I breathe out a sigh of relief. My mind races with everything that could go wrong, while a part of me doesn't care. A part of me just wants him here, in this moment, in this space I've carved out for myself.

I gesture toward the couch where a couple of soft, fluffy blankets are draped over the back. "You can crash there," I say, keeping my tone casual as if this is no big deal. As if inviting a notorious pirate to sleep off our fuckfest in my apartment is something I do all the time.

He nods again, then moves to drop his clothes and boots on the floor by the couch. I can't help but watch as he settles in, his strong, lean form taking up more space than I would have expected. There's a ruggedness to him that seems so out of place here, among the pastels and the delicate touches I've carefully curated. And yet...he fits.

He catches me watching him, and a slow, knowing smile tugs at the corner of his lips. "You sure about this, pixie?" he asks, his voice laced with that infuriating confidence he carries so well.

"Don't push your luck, pirate," I shoot back, the words coming out more playfully than I intended.

I disappear into the bathroom and turn on the shower.

The room begins to steam up and I drop my robe on the floor. Bathing will feel so good.

I can shower off all of the sex and sweat. It doesn't matter at all that Hook is in the next room and my skin still craves his touch.

I don't get the impression the pirate is big into cuddles.

Though the idea of having those broad arms wrapped around me makes me shudder from a different kind of need.

Opening the clear glass door, I step under the rainfall shower head. The steam infuses with the eucalyptus I hung, and I inhale deeply.

My stomach muscles clench with an insistence that runs up to my heart.

You're just hungry, I insist to myself.

I swallow hard, trying to buy into the lie.

Sure, I could use a couple thousand calories after what just happened, but this hunger is deeper. It hits every once in a while, and it has come up with more regular insistence since my last encounter with the cursed pirate.

The gnawing, greedy feeling I've learned to live with. Loneliness.

The truth is, having him here, in my most private space, is terrifying. I've kept everyone at arm's length for so long, guarding this one place that's truly mine.

Spearing my fingers through my long, tangled hair with my special conditioner to help it smooth out, I almost miss the audible creak of the door.

I halt my motions. Hook stands in my bathroom. Through the steamy glass door, there is a blurry expanse of tan skin.

My heart pounds in dull thuds, not just from desire, but from the shock of having someone barge in while I'm vulnerable.

He doesn't say anything. There is an air of hesitance lingering in my small bathroom.

"Yes?" I prompt, with a little impatience.

"I thought maybe..."

Is he actually flustered? What is happening to the world?

Before I let myself think about it, I open the door. Hook steps in, filling the shower. I lose my breath as the scent of his skin and the sex we had intensifies around me in a dizzying cloud.

"Couldn't wait your turn, could you?" I make sure to be

a little flippant. It's only because I'm suddenly angry. Here is this muscular, bad man standing in my shower and I'm resentful I don't get to be held. I don't get to have the afterglow. He's probably in here trying to dick me down again, though we've already hit it a hundred times.

"I like the water," he says in a low, rough voice before turning his face up into the spray. When he looks down at me, droplets cling to his thick lashes. "And I got jealous of it caressing your skin." He runs his fingers softly down my arm, causing a shiver to run through me. I swallow hard.

He leans down and kisses me gently on my lips, and then my cheek before he pulls me into his hard, wet body. "Is this okay?" he murmurs against my ear.

A sob catches in my chest, the embrace so satisfying I nearly explode from gratification.

"Mmmhmm," is all I can get out, looping my arms around his neck, letting him hold me.

And then we just stand there. Hook holds me to him, his blunt wrist slowly swiping up and down the curve of my back in a comforting way. His fingers tangle in my hair. His cheek rests on my head as if he's weary. Suddenly, I am too. Like I've been so strong on my own for so long that I forgot what the safety and strength of someone's arms feel like.

"Thank you," he murmurs in my hair. "Thank you for freeing me. You are an angel. You are a goddess."

Each low rasp-filled word sinks into my flesh, wrapping around my suddenly fragile bones.

With his arm still circling me, he reaches out and opens each soap bottle, giving each a quick sniff. When he inhales my lilac soap, he lets out a low contented groan. Then he grabs my poofy loofah and slathers it in the soap before washing my body.

This lump in my throat's not going away. It fills and

stings me from the inside out. It's filled with these unexplainable feelings I have for the man washing my shoulders with the intensity of someone sculpting a precious piece of art.

It's almost impossible to hold onto the reminder that James T. Hook makes his living off killing my kind.

How could I?

It was one thing to take his money for a job, which even I know is a fucked up thing to do. But this?

I've willingly helped break his curses, fucked him repeatedly, and then invited him into my home.

Panic revs up like an agitated engine in my chest.

Hook's hand stills on my hip, the poofy loofah dripping suds down my thigh. With his other arm, he tilts my chin up to meet his gaze. It's only then I realize I'm holding my breath, and my entire body has tensed. Even my jaw tightens and flexes as my internal conflict rages and roils.

Those deep, piercing eyes bounce between mine. Feeling as if he's probing my thoughts without having to ask a single question, my skin turns itchy from his intense study.

"I didn't kill her," he finally says.

"Wh-what?"

"I didn't murder Sera—" He cuts himself off before he can say the name. "The mermaid."

Jaded doubt spikes in me, but under that is a softer part. A part of me that is desperate to hear more.

Hook doesn't look away as the sponge drops and his fingers curl into my bare, wet hip as if it's the only thing grounding him. "I did want the Waves of Poseidon. I wanted to be taken to the cove, and I began a relationship with her to get there. I wanted her to trust me enough to take me there. But it wasn't all lies. I liked her." He winces as if experiencing some invisible pain. "I never intended to hurt her." The grip on my hip turns near bruising, but I don't squirm away. I'm addicted to hearing every last word that falls from his lips.

It's a spell I'm terrified of breaking, so I stay still, keep silent, on the edge of something I get the sense he's never shared before.

"I knew about the guardian of the cove. I just..." He closes his eyes. "I never thought it would turn on Seraphi-na." His voice turns positively ragged as if raked over sharp gravel. When his eyes open, there is a clarity, a trans-parency that borders on vulnerable. "That was her name. Seraphina."

CHAPTER 24

MERMAID KILLER

HOOK

Seraphina's hair skated between platinum and light iridescent blue. Even her skin had a pale, bluish tint to it from spending so much of her time deep under, far away from the reach of the sun. She was a curious mermaid and when I met her in the oasis of a pool that fed into the ocean, she must have thought it was a coincidence.

It wasn't.

I'd tracked tales of mermaid sightings until I got to the beautiful private pool that had been protected by lush overgrowth and feral animals that ate any trespassers.

My crew stayed aboard the ship while I took my daily journey into the jungle. I almost died on several occasions against fearsome beasts, but I came prepared. I knew how to use a sword and even used the occasional grenade to make passage for myself. I did whatever it took to get past the trials to get to that pool where Seraphina lounged.

She'd been hesitant, fearful at first, but her curiosity won out. I never attempted to interact with her. I simply set up on the opposite side of the pool. I brought a little food and a book. I'd bathe in the water but stuck to my end. Over the course of a week, I proved I wasn't a predator. I was simply another animal at the watering hole.

I still remember the satisfaction that swelled in my chest when her head bobbed up mere feet from mine as I enjoyed my swim.

Gotcha, I thought.

The mermaid asked about the object I kept bringing with me. I explained what a book was. When she wanted to hold it, I told her she couldn't take it underwater, or it would be destroyed.

Still suspicious, she held off a few more days before she pulled herself out of the water enough for her shimmering pink tail to flick and wave in the sunlight as she leaned on her elbows and gingerly turned the pages of the book, unable to read the words.

After that, I'd come back and read to her from the book. It was *The Lady of the Lake* by Sir Walter Scott, a favorite of mine. A narrative poem steeped in Scottish legend and romance, it tells the story of a knight who falls in love with a mysterious lady. The way Seraphina's eyes would round as she watched me while I read, I realized she began to fancy me as her James Fitz-James.

I tried to explain that the Lady of the Lake's lover would return in the end, but Seraphina insisted James Fitz-James was the true romantic hero, and how coincidental we both shared the same name. Then she began to call me James Fitz-James with girlish little giggles.

I didn't encourage her crush, but I didn't discourage it either. So when I began to drop hints about my interest in the Pearlheart Cavern, she only balked a little.

All too soon, she fancied herself Ellen Douglas. Though the anxiety of betraying her family and taking me to the secret sacred cove of her people gave her pause, she agreed to take me to the treasure I sought.

I assured her the item I sought would not be missed. That no one had to know.

I told the crew I would not return for a few days and to enjoy some time off. They knew better than to ask me where I was going.

I packed all I needed in waterproof bags and met Seraphina at our usual lagoon and we swam together. I'm a proficient swimmer, but it put even my muscles to the test, and I had to take breaks on the small float I brought. Seraphina would wait with me, running her fingers through my hair.

Then we came to the Pearlheart Cavern. It was shaped like a skull but that didn't deter me. I needed what was inside.

The Waves of Poseidon.

The gem-like stalagmites overhead were breathtaking and closed clam shells piled around, each holding its own treasure. But I stayed focused. It wasn't long before I pried open the one containing what I sought.

The Waves of Poseidon granted protection from illness, extraordinary strength and speed, and immortality.

I'd be immortal like the Midnight Fae. I would be stronger, with better healing, but I could still be killed if I was dealt a mortal blow. But unlike them, I'd only need to rely on wearing this charm instead of drinking blood. A far better deal.

I knew if I wanted to be the best pirate on the seas, I'd need the power to match my stamina and drive.

When I slipped it over my head, I knew it had all been worth it.

When the power washed over me, I felt invincible.

Stronger than before, healthier than before. Even my reflexes sped up. It was incredible.

Seraphina began to get nervous, her delicate features drawn tight with worry. "James Fitz-James," she whispered, her voice trembling, "We should leave. The Guardian will know we've taken something. The sea will call him."

But before I could respond, the cavern began to tremble. The water around us rippled ominously, and the air grew thick with the scent of decay. Seraphina's hand gripped my arm, her sharp nails digging into my skin.

"We need to go, now!" Her voice was urgent, her eyes wide with fear.

I nodded, swallowing down my own rising panic. The amulet pulsed against my chest. It had taken five years to find, and I didn't plan to lose it as soon as I'd gotten it.

The cavern's entrance loomed ahead, but the water between us and safety suddenly felt like an insurmountable obstacle.

The water around Seraphina darkened as the shadow of something massive moved beneath the surface. A low growl echoed through the cavern, reverberating through the water and sending chills down my spine. Seraphina's eyes widened in terror as the guardian of the cave—a monstrous crocodile god, far larger than any beast I'd ever encountered—emerged from the depths.

Its scales were as black as the abyss, and its eyes glowed with an unnatural, malevolent light.

"James Fitz-James, we must leave!" Seraphina's voice was filled with a desperation that mirrored my own.

But the Guardian was faster. It lunged toward us, jaws snapping shut just inches from where Seraphina hovered in the water. Without thinking, I pushed her aside, shoving her back toward the entrance as I tried to draw the Guardian's attention.

"Go!" I shouted, my voice hoarse with fear. I sloshed through the shallow water to position myself between Seraphina and the monstrous creature. The Guardian roared again, the sound reverberating through the cave and rattling my bones.

Seraphina hesitated, her eyes filled with a mix of fear and guilt. But there was no time for second thoughts. I barely had time to dive out of the way as the Guardian lunged again, its jaws snapping shut with a deafening crack where I'd been standing.

"Seraphina, swim!" I shouted again, this time with more urgency.

She finally moved, diving beneath the water, her shimmering pink tail flicking as she swam toward the entrance. I followed her as best I could, the water slowing me down as I tried to keep up. The Guardian's massive tail whipped through the water, sending waves crashing into me and throwing me off-balance. I fell back, gasping as the water closed over my head.

When I surfaced, sputtering and desperate, I saw Seraphina struggling against the current, the Guardian closing in on her.

Without a second thought, I launched myself toward the creature, my sword drawn. I swung wildly, the blade catching the Guardian's snout and drawing a thin line of blood.

The beast roared in pain, its eyes narrowing as it turned its full attention to me. It lunged again, this time faster than before, and I knew I couldn't dodge it. The massive jaws clamped down on my hand, sword and all, the pain blinding and all-consuming as my bones first shattered under the pressure. Then every nerve ending in my body screamed as the appendage was separated from my body.

"James!" Seraphina's scream was barely audible over the sound of the creature's roar.

My strength waned, the amulet's power struggling to keep me conscious. With my other hand, I grabbed a dagger from my belt and jammed it into the crocodile's nose. It released what was left of my wrist, thrashing in anger. The mangled limb mocked me. Immortality, at a price.

The dagger wouldn't put the Guardian off for long, so I fumbled for the small grenade at my belt—the last of my explosives. In desperation, I yanked the pin with my teeth and shoved the device into the beast's mouth. I dove away, swimming as fast as I could to put distance between us.

The explosion was deafening, the force of it engulfing me in violent waves. I was sinking, my vision fading as the water closed over me.

When I surfaced again, gasping for air, I saw the Guardian retreating, blood trailing behind it as it vanished into the depths. But there was no relief, no sense of victory.

Seraphina floated in the water, her body limp, her unseeing eyes wide open. The blast had caught her in its wake.

"Seraphina," I choked out, my voice breaking as I struggled toward her. But I already knew it was too late. Even so, I pulled the necklace over my head and put it over hers, willing it to give her life. But the light had gone out of her, and no amount of magic could bring her back.

My hand was gone, a bloody, mangled limb now. The life was draining out of me with every passing second. But the pain of my injuries was nothing compared to the agony of losing Seraphina.

I barely remember the moments that followed. Somehow, I made it out of the cave, dragging myself onto the shore where my crew eventually found me. They hauled me to the ship, their faces grim as they took in the sight of their captain, broken and battered.

The Waves of Poseidon still hung around my neck, but it felt like a hollow victory. I had gained the power I sought but at great cost. My hand, but more importantly, Seraphina was gone, and with her, the last remnants of my humanity.

As the *Jolly Roger* sailed away from the cursed cove, I stared out at the endless horizon, knowing that I would never escape the darkness that now consumed me. The amulet had promised me strength and immortality, but it would always be a reminder of my mistakes and regret.

CHAPTER 25

THE HATE IN MY HEART

"I've never told anyone this before," Hook confesses to me, staring at the ceiling of my bedroom.

I'd moved us from the shower when it went cold, though Hook didn't seem to notice. We slipped underneath the covers of my bed, and he told me the rest of what happened to Seraphina.

My fingers flutter over his skin as I anxiously listen to his story.

"Seraphina's kin tracked me down. They held me responsible for her death. They should," he adds darkly.

"Why didn't they try to take the Waves of Poseidon back?" I ask just above a whisper.

He shakes his head. "They wanted me to suffer. The three mermaids cursed me knowing I'd never leave the ocean, that I would always love what could never love me back. It's a special kind of hell." At that, he tilts his head down to look at me. I don't understand the emotion crossing his face. As if something else causes him pain. "And you've freed me from it."

Hook leans down and kisses me so softly, so tenderly that my heart breaks in my chest.

When he draws back, there is a slight smile on his face. Before now, I've only ever seen that cocky smirk of his. This one makes him look younger, and I get a glimpse of that young man who sought treasure at any cost. What a beautiful, bold idiot.

His smile fades. "Though maybe you shouldn't have. Perhaps you should have refused and forced me to continue my hellish existence."

I lick my lips, trying to quell how bothered I feel at that prospect.

"Why didn't you?"

"What?" I ask, emerging from under the mire of my own feelings.

"Why didn't you refuse me? I realize the first time I hit you in your pride, but the next, you knew what power burst would likely happen. That you were helping a bad man." There is almost a tease in his last words, but he's also being so very serious.

I shift and turn onto my side away from him. Hook simply molds himself to the back of me, his arm wrapping around my waist, pulling me in.

Squeezing my eyes shut, I try to ignore the answer rolling around in my mouth.

After a long moment, he says, "It's okay. You don't have to tell me." Then he kisses my closed wings.

Heat shivers through the delicate veins, building an inferno in me.

He continues to kiss and trace his tongue along them until I'm on my stomach and they extend out for his consideration. The way his tongue and lips trace the thin layers of chitin has my hips grinding into the bed, the ache growing between my legs. There is also the ache in my chest that needs and wants more than just physical gratification. I shut my eyes against my heart's request.

Hook drags the tip of his tongue down the base of my spine before grabbing hold of one globe of my ass. Using his other wrist to nudge the other side, he maneuvers me until I'm on my knees and spread entirely to his view.

"Fucking beautiful." His words land on my sex in a hot breath, causing my wings and inner muscles to flutter. I'm fully exposed, and it makes me feel so very vulnerable, yet so very fucking turned on.

He buries his face in my pussy, nose pushing between my cheeks as he licks gently at my lower lips. I arch and grind into his probing tongue, riding out my pleasure. I'm still sore from earlier but his ministrations are soft and gentle.

"James," I gasp, when he slips a finger inside of me, pumping in an unhurried pace that floods my brain and body with endorphins.

Instead of the furious, frantic need to get ourselves and each other off, the ruthless Captain Hook licks and strokes me for an impossibly long time. As if he has all the time in the world and needs nothing more from me than to just let him touch. Let him taste.

After what feels like an eternity, ecstasy vibrates through me from my temples to my toes in a wash of pleasure.

It leaves me panting, and us tangled in each other. Hook doesn't push me any further. He doesn't enter me, he simply curls back around me, though his cock is hard against my hip.

I can't keep running from the truth—not with the way

he's looking at me now, his eyes searching mine for answers I've tried to avoid.

"I didn't refuse because..." I start, my voice barely above a whisper. "Because I wanted to be around you."

The pirate blinks, clearly taken aback by my admission. "You wanted to be around me?" he echoes, his tone a mix of surprise and something softer, almost tender.

I nod, swallowing hard. "I want to say it was because I saw something better inside you, that I believed in the good man I thought you could be. But that wasn't it. Not really. The truth is...I just wanted to be near *you*."

His gaze darkens, but there's no anger there. Instead, there's a flicker of something that looks a lot like under-standing. "You mean you wanted to be near a villain?"

"Not just a villain," I correct, turning my head to look at him fully. "You're both dark and light, James. You're complicated, flawed, and dangerous. But you're real. I've had my fill of perfect men on pedestals. Peter...he was up there in the light, where everything looked clean and good. But you, you're in the dirt, where life is messy and raw. I don't think I'd ever trust anyone who wasn't a bit of both."

He's silent for a moment, his expression unreadable. Then he lets out a low, almost bitter laugh. "So, you're saying you like your men dirty?"

I smile, though it's tinged with sadness. "I'm saying I like my men real."

Hook looks at me and for the first time, I think he truly sees me—not just the pixie who has been taunting him or the tattoo artist with a chip on her shoulder, but as someone who understands what it's like to straddle the line between light and dark.

Sure, I may not go around stealing and murdering, but I have hate in my heart. For Pan, for Wendy, for the crappy

Boston drivers, for people who abuse animals. Sometimes I feel shitty for being petty or resentful or pissy at the world around me, but something about Hook makes it okay to be exactly what I am. Like proof the world does suck, but it can be conquered.

"There's more to it, though," I continue, feeling the weight of what I'm about to say. "You helped that little girl. You helped Seraphina. Even if you didn't do it for the right reasons, you still did it. Like I said, you also possess light. I think you need someone to remind you of that, or at the very least, remember it for you when you forget."

His expression softens, and for a moment I see the man he could be, the man he wants to be—but then, just as quickly, the mask slips back into place.

"I'm married to the ocean, Tink," he says, his voice rough with emotion. "I can't landlock myself. The sea is in my blood, in my bones. I couldn't leave it any more than I could stop breathing."

"And I couldn't leave Boston," I admit, feeling the sting of the truth in my words. "I couldn't leave my clients, my life on land. This place is my home, James." His expression softens when I say his name. "There's something about this place, about the roots I've put down here, that I can't just walk away from. Maybe it's being near my old tree, or maybe it's just me, but...I'm bound to this city, just like you're bound to the sea."

Our lives are too different. We'd smother each other, steal each other's purpose, trying to hold on too tightly to whatever *this* is.

"There was a time when I believed in Peter Pan's world," a lyrical musing enters my voice, "where everything was an adventure, and innocence was something to cling to. But innocence is a luxury, and Boston's taught me that life isn't about never growing up—it's about surviving, about finding your place even after everything you once believed in dies."

"We're survivors," he says as if mulling it over.

I nod.

We both fall silent, the reality of our situation settling between us like a lead weight.

"Well, that's that?" he asks quietly, his voice laced with a resignation that tugs at my heart.

I sigh and drop my head back. "Guess so."

We lie there in silence, our bodies still pressed together.

Then he tilts my head toward his and kisses me. The languid pace allows heat to build at a lazy yet pressing rate. Then I'm climbing onto his lap and lowering myself onto his hardness as we make love in slow thrusts. He tells me I'm beautiful, a treasure like no other, that I deserve better.

My wings release pixie dust until the glinting particles swirl and sparkle around us, catching every bit of sunshine streaming into the windows. I whisper that I see him. He can't hide from me, no matter how he tries.

Staring into each other's eyes we both break and shudder with release, clinging to each other. It's all we can do since all we want to do is cling to more time. But in my apartment, the *tik-tik-tik* of the clock is a constant reminder that time runs on no matter what. And our time is almost up.

It's not the ending I want, but it's the one we have. And for now, it's enough.

CHAPTER 26
ONE SUNNY DAY
TINK

Every time there are storms, I think of him. Something yawns open with need and loneliness for a certain muscular, long-haired pirate.

I used to be more present with my clients, chatting easily. Now, I've retreated inside myself. I can still paste on a smile, but part of me is unreachable, like I'm always somewhere else.

It's only been two months since Hook left, curse-free and able to go back to the sea he loves, and live the way he's always wanted.

When the door chimes on this particular sunny day, I don't turn around with any real anticipation.

"I'm closing up," I call out, cleaning the station where I finished my last tattoo.

"Well, that's a shame. I was hoping to get my belly button pierced."

The familiar raspy voice shoots a jolt through my spine until it's ramrod straight.

It's almost like a dream as I turn around to find sunrays

surrounding Hook, as if the world at large didn't know the devil was on my doorstep.

Not that I care much for what the world thinks of James T. Hook right now. My heart slams into my ribcage with anticipation, though I'm not sure what it could be expecting.

"Sir, if you want your belly button pierced, you'll have to come back tomorrow," I explain, biting the inside of my cheek to suppress the smile.

Hook looks good. His hair is pulled back into a low knot with messy strands falling around his face. I marvel that he's one of the few who can pull off that look with such masculine swagger and appeal. The jagged scar on his throat has healed even more, so I can barely see the thin line.

His eyes remain dark, stormy, intent, and completely fixed on me. It's hard to breathe, caught in his sights. My wings flutter of their own accord, unable to hold the delight at bay.

Calm down, Tink. He's not staying. It doesn't matter.

"Ah well, that's a shame." Hook snaps his fingers in disappointment with a half-smirk. "Well then, maybe you can help me with something else."

I'm not sure if it's part of our game, or because I really do enjoy being a brat. I cross my arms over my chest. "It'll cost you."

He chuckles, and it's a low, rough sound. "I'd expect nothing else." Then he holds out a hand. "I want to show you something."

My fingers itch to slip into his, but my heart sends a couple of warning beats to my brain.

You are vulnerable. He could hurt you. You are an independent fairy, and it needs to stay that way.

The smirk falls away from his eyes as if he knows I'm pulling my defenses around me. "Ten minutes. And then after that, you never have to see me again if you don't like."

My hand slips into his.

THE POISON APPLE won't open for another couple of hours, so I'm surprised when Hook opens the front door and leads me inside the bar.

"What are we doing here?" I ask. On the way over, we chatted about nothing and everything.

The shop is doing well.

It has been particularly sunny lately.

Hook has retained the same crew for a while now. It's been good.

I'm hungry for any information I can get, even though it's only scraps.

Has he met someone new? Made a life with her now that he's curse-free? Surely this visit is nothing more than a professional call.

Despite my reason, my heart thumps insistently with hope.

In the bar, I'm surrounded by the familiar scent of aged wood, flowers, and something sweet lingering in the air.

It's quiet—the kind of quiet that feels sacred, like the world outside has paused just for us. Light shines down from the skylights, giving the Poison Apple a very different feel from the usual moody lighting and stars of night overhead.

"What's this about, Hook?" I ask, trying to keep my voice steady.

My mouth sours instantly. I wanted to call him James, but I have no right to use his name so intimately.

He doesn't answer right away. Instead, he guides me to the far corner of the bar where a small, round table has been set up. On it, sitting in the center like a crown jewel is a small potted plant. At first, it looks like nothing special—just a sapling, its leaves a bright, vibrant green. But as I get closer, something stirs inside me. A warmth, a familiarity that's as comforting as it is terrifying.

I gasp, my wings fluttering uncontrollably. "Is that—"

Hook nods, his eyes never leaving my face. "It's from your tree, Tink. The original one."

My breath catches in my throat as I reach out to touch the leaves, feeling the faint pulse of magic that radiates from the tiny plant.

It's different from the magic I remember, but it's still connected to me in a way that makes my chest tighten with fierce nostalgia.

"How. . ." I whisper, unable to tear my eyes away from the sapling.

"I made a trade with the tree," Hook says quietly. "The Waves of Poseidon for a seed. Magic demands a trade, after all."

I blink up at him, my mind reeling. My eyes go to the necklaces hanging from his neck, and sure enough, the waves are conspicuously absent. "You traded your immortality for this?"

He shrugs as if it's nothing, but I can see the weight of the decision in his eyes. My stomach shoots up then back down as if riding an out-of-control roller coaster.

"I couldn't stand the thought of you not having a place that felt like home," he goes on. "I know it's not the same, but...maybe you could have a new one. One that's just yours."

My fingers tremble as I trace the delicate leaves, feeling the connection between the sapling and myself grow stronger with each passing second. It recognizes me, just as I recognize it. It's a piece of my past, something I thought I'd lost forever, now growing right in front of me.

"It will take time before it's fully grown," Hook continues. "But I've been taking care of it on the ship, making sure it's hearty enough to survive. I wanted to give it to you when I knew it wouldn't die on you. I wanted to give you something that could be yours." His words come out with the vulnerability of a boy seeking approval but worried he won't get it.

I swallow hard, emotions swirling inside me in a chaotic mix of disbelief, gratitude, and a strong, spreading warmth that quickly overtakes my chest. "Why would you do this for me?"

He steps closer, his eyes locking onto mine with an intensity that makes my heart skip a beat. "The Waves of Poseidon had been my anchor, the thing that kept me chained to the life of a pirate, of a man bound to the sea. But giving it up—for you, for this sapling—was like shedding the last of my old skin. I'm still a pirate, still drawn to the wild freedom of the ocean, but I'm not the man I was when I first put that amulet on. And maybe, just maybe, I can be something more now. I could come ashore for a while, and you could come on the ship with me. We'd take the tree, and I've..." He lets out an incredulous laugh as he blushes and pushes his hair back as if embarrassed. The roller coaster my stomach is riding is heading directly down and I am falling, falling, falling before he's finished the sentence. "I've even set up my cabin to be full of plants, so you'd feel at home."

I stare at him, my mind struggling to process everything he's saying.

This man, this pirate who has spent his life taking and conquering, is offering me something I thought I could never have again—a fairy's home. A place where my pixie dust can collect and settle.

Hook takes my hand in his, his grip strong and steady. Fae lords, there's nothing like the feel of his completely calloused palm. "I may be a bad man, Tink, but with you, I could be a little good. I'll love you more than anyone else ever could because I know treasure when I see it. And I have to have you. I'm a pirate. It's what I do."

The sincerity in his voice, the raw honesty in his eyes, shake me to my core. I've spent so long building walls around myself, keeping everyone at a distance, but with Hook...those walls crumble. He's offering me everything I've ever wanted, everything I've been too afraid to hope for.

But can I take it?

CHAPTER 27

THE BIG MAGIC WOOD

HOOK

As Tink stares at the sapling, her eyes wide and filled with something I can't quite place, my heart thunders in my chest. I've faced down beasts, battled storms, and cheated death more times than I can count, but standing here, waiting for her to decide, feels like the most dangerous thing I've ever done.

If she says no, if she turns away, I don't know what I'll do. I'd give up everything for her—cut off my other hand if she asked. I just need her to say yes.

The months of preparation and the time it's taken me to learn how to care for plants so they thrive in an old salty pirate's ship took an embarrassingly long time. But she's worth it. She's worth every book I read, and every small plant I killed before I was confident enough to plant the acorn her tree gave me for the Waves of Poseidon.

The silence stretches on, heavy and suffocating, and I can feel my control slipping. The need to reach out, to touch her, to pull her into my arms and never let go, is almost unbearable. But I force myself to stay still, to give her the space she needs to make her decision.

I can't take her.

She has to give herself to me. Which is the most counterintuitive thing to a pirate there can be.

After what feels like an eternity, she turns to face me, her expression unreadable. My heart skips a beat, my breath catching in my throat as I wait for her answer.

Then, to my utter relief, she cracks a smile—a small, wicked little smile. "You're making a terrible villain right now, you know that?"

Air rushes out of my lungs, a smirk spreading across my face.

She steps closer, her fingers trailing over the scars on my chest. For a moment, she doesn't say anything, just traces the marks like she's mapping the pieces of me she's still trying to figure out. Then she looks up, her eyes locking onto mine, and there's a seriousness there that hits me like a punch.

"You know, I've spent years chasing something—a place, a feeling. Something that felt like home," she says, her voice low, thoughtful. "I thought I'd make it in Boston, in my shop, with my clients. And I did, in a way. But it was never quite enough. There was always this gnawing emptiness, like no matter how many roots I put down, I was still floating, still searching."

Tink's words twist something inside me, something I've never let myself acknowledge—maybe because I've been running too. From what, I'm not sure. But I know that look in her eyes like I know my own reflection.

"And then you show up," she continues, her voice gaining a bit of that edge I love so much, "with your cursed tattoos and your dangerous charm, turning my world upside down. And I've been trying to figure out why, when you left, I couldn't go back to the way things were. Why it felt like the color had drained out of the world."

She pauses, her fingers stopping their tracing to rest over my heart like she's anchoring herself to me. "It's not just the tree," she says finally, her voice barely above a whisper. "It's you, James. You make me feel like I'm not floating anymore. Like maybe I don't need a place to put down roots because you...you might be my home."

The admission is raw like she's peeling back a layer she's kept hidden even from herself. And damn if it doesn't make something break open inside me too.

But I can't resist pushing her buttons, even now. "So," I say, trying to keep my tone light, teasing, even though my chest is about to burst, "does this mean I should give the plant away?"

Her eyes narrow, a dangerous glint in them as she smacks my arm—hard. "You try it, and I'll pierce your belly button and give you a big ol' tramp stamp of a butterfly with hearts."

I chuckle, the sound rumbling up from deep in my chest as I pull her close again, burying my face in the crook of her neck. "Not a chance, love. Not a chance in hell."

TASTING RED

Want more of the Lost Girls? Enjoy this peek into book 1 of Tasting Red

"Why did you call me here?" I ask, though I know perfectly well why the grizzled old son of a bitch sent for me. I spin the titanium ring around my forefinger with my thumb.

He frowns under his thick beard, across from me at the wooden table. He pushes a pint of ale over before grabbing his own. I don't pick up the mug, but the man shrugs and takes a swig.

How did I end up here? For most of my life, I've lived on my terms with no consideration for anyone else. Not even the women I sometimes let in my bed. I follow the jobs that bring the most money and that has served me perfectly well until now.

"It's been a long time, Brexley," he says.

Nineteen years, if one were counting. And for nineteen years, I've felt the ghostly shackle, tying me to someone else. Nearly two-thirds of my life, waiting for the shoe to drop.

"Not long enough," I say gruffly, finally grabbing the mug and taking a healthy swallow of the stuff. I hate to admit the shit is good. So I don't.

I've done everything I could to be free of social ties. There is no place for me among mage, man, or fae. But today is the day my only marker is called.

I owe one being a favor in this entire world and he has summoned me here to the musty backroom of his tavern. Boxes pile high around the room, surrounding us. He named the joint *Sam's*, though his name is Jameson. I never asked who he named it after, and I still won't ask.

The drizzle kicks up a heavy mist that clings to the windows. The cold seeps its way into my bones despite my knit sweater and leather jacket. On a shitty day like this, I'd normally be at home by the fire with a book. But this old son of a bitch has me by the balls.

"You owe me, Brexley," Jameson starts, as if he expects a fight.

I wipe my mouth with the back of my hand. "I'm aware, you old bastard. Just tell me what you want so we can get this over with."

His calloused fingers drum on the manilla folder next to him before sliding it over. "I need you to take care of her."

His tone tells me he doesn't mean take her out for lunch and shopping. He must have been keeping tabs on me to know what kind of business I'm in now. Or maybe he's just a sadistic son of a bitch, and I could be a florist and he'd still give me the same mission.

I push the mug away, despite wanting more. Drinking won't make this problem disappear. But once my only debt is paid, I won't have anything hanging over me. I'll truly be free.

I flip the folder open to a picture and a single page of

details: name, occupation, home addresses. But I didn't need any of that info. I instantly recognize the older woman in the photo. I've seen her many times—on billboards, commercials, packages of food, enamel pins that people stick on their jackets.

A dry snort escapes me. "You've got to be joking."

The old bastard doesn't crack a smile, doesn't move a muscle.

Fuck me.

I run a hand through my already unruly silver hair. "Grandma. You want me to go after Grandma from 'Grandma's House?' The face of the most popular household brand, and one of the most powerful witches known to the world?"

Jameson repeats himself in slow, steady words. "You owe me." Coiled tension is locked up behind his dark eyes and in the set of his broad shoulders. Blood lust shines out from his face. This is business from his past. But I don't ask questions, and I'm not about to start now.

I study him, observing how he's changed since I last saw him. Even more gray strands pepper his black hair and beard. His scowl has only deepened with the years, multiplying the lines at the corners of his eyes. He must be nearing his fifties, but under his flannel shirt vest is a body still packed with the sturdy muscles of a heavyweight boxer.

Once upon a time, I considered this man to be like a father to me. He quickly dispelled me of that notion with an unholy vengeance. He taught me the truth. Dependence is death. Don't buy into the lie. You don't need others to survive in this world. It is a gilded lie that ends with getting stabbed in the back.

Or, in my case, a set of claws raked across my face.

But finally, I'm given the opportunity to dissolve my last tie to another being, and this is my chance. As one of the most beloved celebrity icons, this also may be my chance to get killed.

My fingers wrap around the cold handle of the mug, suddenly thirsty. "She won't be easy to get to. And afterward, I'll be hunted like an animal."

His chair creaks with a loud groan as he leans back with a smirk. I've already accepted his terms. "Good thing you're used to it."

So he does know my business.

I shoot him a cutting look over the edge of the mug as I swallow the rest of the amber liquid.

"After all," he folds his arms across his chest, "you are the Big Bad Wolf."

My grin is half-grimace. "And that is very bad news for grandmas right now."

~

Head to Holly's website https://hollyroberds.com to find out what happens when Red and the Big Bad collide at grandma's house

WANT A FREE BOOK?

Want the matching ebook for FREE!
Hooking Tink—my sizzling novella starring Tinkerbell and
Captain Hook—is part of my bestselling Lost Girls series...
and you can download it free right now! Visit my website
https://hollyroberds.com/hooking-tink/ to grab your
copy now!

LOVE THIS BOOK?
ENJOY MORE BY THIS AUTHOR

Vivien woke up with no memories and a terrible thirst for blood.

The Grim Reaper must destroy all blood suckers.

The reaper dogs just want to get pets and loves in between fetching the souls for the Afterlife.

Read this COMPLETE trilogy and you'll laugh, you'll cry, you'll absolutely die.

Vegas Immortals: Death & the Last Vampire

LOVE THIS BOOK?

*Available on Audio and Kindle Unlimited

Acknowledgments

This creative take on Hook is very much the fault of my friend Shannon who dead-eye looked at me and said 'take the hook off' when I claimed I didn't know how to incorporate that particular part into the story.

Bruce, you backed her up and brought us 'yeah, have her wristed instead of fisted.'

And then to l'husbun who swooped in at the end pointing out that very much makes Hook handicapable. I

have the weirdest most unhinged circle of people. Thank god.

A massive thank you to my assistants, Leah Crowell and Tara Volpenhein. I can't stress enough what a massive impact you two have made on my business, my time, and my well being.

Thank you to Sarah Urquhart for the days we sat (virtually) on my deck pounding out the words in between being distracted by the bird's nest in my flower basket.

Thank you to my editors Theresa Paolo, Havoc Archives & Athena Franks, thanks for sticking with my unhinged ass and cleaning up my messes.

To my special reader fan group, *Holly's Hellions* – you support me in ways I can't express deep enough gratitude for.

To my Patrons – how dare you support the saga of what was entitled 'the Nub-ening' that chronicles the making of this novella. I love you, freaks.

Thank you to l'husbun, for offering up your arm (without question) so I could encircle my fingers around your wrist and then walking away with a rather surprising measurement and no explanation.

A Letter from the Author

A Letter from the Author

Dear Reader,

Thank you for reading!

I shamelessly hope to have hooked on the Lost Girls in the hopes you'll come explore the world with me and come hang with Red, Goldie, Cinder and more! More Lost Girls are coming down the pipeline, and I can't wait to find out which one resonates with you the most.

Want to make sure you never miss a release or any bonus content I have coming down the pipeline? Make sure to join my Patreon: Holly Roberds Books

And definitely sign up for Holly's Hotspot, my newsletter, and I'll send you a FREE ebook right away!

You can also find me on my website www.hollyroberds.com and I hang out on social media.

Instagram: http://instagram.com/authorhollyroberds

Facebook: www.facebook.com/hollyroberdsauthorpage/

And closest to my black heart is my reader fan group,

Holly's Hellions. Become a Hellion. Raise Hell. www.facebook.com/groups/hollyshellions/

Cheers!

Holly Roberds

ABOUT THE AUTHOR

Holly started out writing Buffy the Vampire Slayer and Terminator romantic fanfiction before spinning off into her own fantastic worlds with bitey MCs and heart wrenching climaxes as well as other errr climaxes...

Holly is a Colorado girl to her core but is only outdoorsy in that she likes drinking on patios in Denver.

She lives with her ever-supportive husband who feeds her, keeps her sane and gives the best hugs when she faces down her own personal hell aka edits.

For more sample chapters, news, and more, visit www. hollyroberds.com

www.ingramcontent.com/pod-product-compliance
Lightning Source LLC
Chambersburg PA
CBHW060450300726

48975CB00008B/2458